Will Tripp

Pissed Off Attorney at Law

Harry Stein

WILL TRIPP
PISSED OFF ATTORNEY AT LAW

a StoneThread publication

Printed in the United Stated of America

* * * * *

Disclaimer

This is a work of fiction, a product of the author's imagination. Any resemblance or similarity to any actual events or persons, living or dead, is purely coincidental. Although the author and publisher have made every effort to ensure there are no errors, inaccuracies, omissions, or inconsistencies herein, any slights of people, places, or organizations are unintentional.

* * * * *

Credits

Cover photo courtesy Getty Images
Initial cover design by Dane Low, Ebook Launch

Final cover design by Harvey Stanbrough
www.harveystanbrough.com

Interior formatted by Debora Lewis
arenapublishing.org

ISBN-13: 978-1492737629
ISBN-10: 1492737623

Will Tripp: Pissed Off Attorney at Law

There's an excellent reason this story does not begin in a bar. There are only two such establishments close to Bennett Tripp's home in the now-famous college town of South Chester, New York, and he was not about to patronize either.

One, Seventh Heaven, was owned by the woman with whom his wife and child had just taken up residence. The other, Rick's Place, had long before permanently offended the one person on earth he could always count on, his brother Will.

That evening Bennett was counting on Will more than ever. Earlier, hearing the sound of Bennett's voice on the phone, Will had announced he was dropping everything and heading over.

"I'm all right," Bennett said. "Don't bother."

"Yeah, and I'm doing Scarlett Johansson with my foot-long hose," Will replied. "Sit tight, little brother—just wait till I get there to break out the rat poison."

It generally took Will a good two hours to reach South Chester from his Yonkers law office, but tonight he made it in ninety minutes, and that included a stop at a liquor store. Emerging from his custom-altered 2010 Escalade, he hoisted both hands over his head in greeting, a brown paper bag in each.

Waiting on the porch steps, Bennett waved vaguely and rose unsteadily to his feet.

"Asshole," observed Will warmly, "started without me." He set down the bags in turn. "Scotch. Vodka."

Normally not much for drinking, Bennett had already had three Buds. "Don't worry, I got plenty of room."

"I'm disappointed—you really don't look so bad," Will said, smiling, and threw his arms around his brother's waist.

"I try." Having earlier presided over his senior seminar on Fluid Mechanics, he was still wearing his corduroy jacket, though there was now a large spot of spilt beer on the front.

Will disengaged. "Look at the bright side—at least she didn't take the house."

"Not yet," Bennett said, turning to trudge up the porch steps, the floorboards moaning with every step.

Will followed. "Oh, boy," he said, rubbing his hands together in anticipation. "Let's hope she tries!"

* * *

"I swear, it's like getting castrated." So deep in his armchair he was more lying than sitting, Bennett reached uncertainly for his glass on the nearby table.

From his perch on a stool across the room, Will shot him a look. "Waaah, waaah, waaah. How long you gonna go on with this?"

"Castrated with a dull butter knife. Long as I please!"

"Christ, if you're just gonna make yourself another victim, do it on your own time!"

If there's one thing Will hated, it was victims. He'd built his entire career on fighting victims or, as he put it, "defending the real victims." By this he meant everyone getting screwed by out-of-control do-gooders, dull-witted bureaucrats and the terminally PC, from doctors faced with losing their practices to specious malpractice claims, to employers constrained from firing even the most incompetent and dishonest employees, to hapless saps busted for smoking in public.

He'd decided on this course back in law school, nearly twenty years before. He had paid his way through school working weekends and summers at the aforementioned Rick's Place, nightly donning his padded suit and crash helmet to get tossed by happily inebriated customers into a bank of mattresses, under the name Iron Will.

Need it be mentioned Will's a dwarf? Because you surely already knew that if you've followed the events leading to the mystifying end of Francine Grabler, Chester College's renowned professor of Advanced Oppression Studies.

The point is, Will had never had such a terrific job, great money and even better psychic rewards. "I was a fucking *athlete*!" he later opined. But then the human rights activists got involved, standing up for—he always made sneer quotes with his stubby fingers—"'the Little People.' *Little People!* Screw that, we're *dwarves*!"

Indeed, as he insistently pointed out to the smug and ignorant, they *had* to be dwarves. "You can't toss a damn midget; you don't have the right weight/balance ratio!"

One night, a couple dozen of the do-gooders showed up to picket the place, and the owner, Rick, instantly folded, terrified the bastards would get some lily-livered pol to suspend his liquor license. He gave Will his walking papers, then helped finance an ordinance mandating a $5000 fine and up to six months for anyone caught hurling a dwarf within town limits. He won praise in the town weekly and an award from the ACLU.

Meanwhile, Will's new job—inspecting the interiors of municipal sewage pipes—paid a third of the old one, without factoring in the lost glory.

All these years later, Rick was still high on Will's Get-Even list.

"Look at the bright side," he said to Bennett. "At least you don't have to put up with all her New Age crap anymore."

"I thought you liked Laura."

"I did. But know what? I'm *judgmental.*" He let the wonderful word, transformed by the proudly sensitive into a pejorative, hang in the air a moment. "She's a jerk, that wife of yours. And I don't say that just because she turned out to be a rug muncher."

Bennett threw up a hand. "Hey, no, stop!"

Will shot him a sad smile. What could he do? The poor sap had been marinating in the PC stew of American higher education for so long he couldn't think straight. "Hey, I don't mind a bit. Matter of fact, that generally elevates a woman in my esteem."

"All right, then," allowed Bennett uncertainly.

"Only, Christ, what's this country's coming to when you can't speak the truth even to a guy who's just taken a shiv to his nuts? Your wife suddenly decides after ten years she's bored and needs her freedom? And doesn't give a goddamn how it messes up the kid?"

"She's a good mother, Will. It's me she doesn't want...."

"Waaah, waaah, waaah. Yeah, right, that's why she's after full custody of Casey. Know what she is? A selfish bitch on skates! No embarrassment, no accountability." He paused. "A moral black hole. Say it."

"You're wrong, it's so much more complicated than that." Suddenly Bennett looked like he might actually start to cry. In the several days since his four year-old daughter had moved to Barbara Ann's place with her mother, she'd gone monosyllabic on him, and he had nightmare visions of her shutting him out for good. "A lot more complicated," he repeated softly.

This bid for sympathy failed to have the desired effect. "Just listen to yourself! I'm not sure I wouldn't leave you too!"

"Yeah, well great... I appreciate all the help."

"You want me to represent you or not?"

"I know what you're trying to do, Will, and I love you for it."

"Right, I love you too. Now say it!" He paused. "I need to know you'll do what I'll need you to do."

"Fine," he said softly. "She's a black hole."

"Say it like you mean it. A *moral* black hole."

"A moral black hole."

"Louder!"

"A moral black hole!"

Will nodded. "You got all your financial records in order?"

"Kept them in my office, like you said."

"Good." Will hopped off his stool and gave his brother a quick hug. "We'll talk tomorrow." He started for the door, then paused. "Your colleagues know?"

"That she's left me? Of course not."

"If I were you, I'd use it."

Bennett looked at him quizzically.

"To get other women. Trust me, pity can be a tool. They're *educators*. Empathy is job one."

* * * * *

"Your Honor, may I approach?"

State Supreme Court Justice Carol Siegel peered down at Will over her half-glasses. "You may."

"Your Honor, I'm really not comfortable humiliating a child."

Though her other features remained studiously neutral, her eyes flashed bemusement; it wasn't the first time she'd had Will Tripp in her White Plains courtroom, and she knew sensitivity wasn't his long suit. "I sympathize, Counselor. I'm sure you'll exercise restraint."

"On the other hand, if you throw out this ridiculous case right now...."

At that, she couldn't help but smile. "Enough Will... just continue your cross."

Turning away, Will caught his client's attention and shot him a grin intended to induce confidence. It didn't work. A useful and productive citizen, a wholesaler of pet supplies whose last speeding ticket had been as a twenty-two year old, even now Warren Lucas seemed to scarcely believe the position he was in: sitting in this spanking new, state-of-the-art courtroom, a financial Sword of Damocles hanging over his head. And for what? The damn kid had snuck into *his* yard. Swung on *his* rope swing. How was it *his* fault that she'd jumped off and broken her ankle? In fact, when her parents first started making noises about a lawsuit, he'd threatened to sue them for trespass. Or slander. Something! But no. How could he know that under New York's Child Omnibus Protection Act, otherwise known as Jao's Law, after the 14-year old Thai lad who tried practicing his tight rope walking skills on the Long Island Railroad's Third Rail, that it was the responsibility of the property owner to post to warnings in multiple languages within forty feet of any potential danger accessible to children under eighteen? The Moses had sued for $14.8 million—the amount a helpful accountant had surmised their ballet-prodigy daughter stood to have earned had her career not been curtailed by the injury—and until he found Will, he'd lived in dread that he would have to pay a good chunk of it.

Even now, sitting beside Will's wheelchair-bound associate Marjorie Spivak at the defense table, he had the look of a hunted animal.

"Now, then," Will said amiably, turning back to face Jodie Moses on the stand, "you were telling us about Miss Waring, Katie's ballet instructor at the—"

"Waring Academy," she said coolly. "In Armonk, New York. Soon after she started there, Ms. Waring told us Katie's gifted. *Extremely* gifted. One of her *most* gifted. Ever." A beat, then sadly. "Or *was.*"

"I see. And by chance would you know off-hand how many of Miss Waring's pupils have gone on to The City Ballet in New York?"

She looked only momentarily uncertain before answering with haughty distain. "No. And I don't see that it matters."

"Or the ABT—the American Ballet Theater?"

"I *know* what it is!"

Abruptly, the phone in Will's shirt pocket begin to vibrate—the violent vibration, signaling a distress call from one of his handful of intimates. He turned away from the witness stand and, unseen by the judge and witness, whipped it out for a quick glance. *BIG trouble, need you NOW—B*, read Bennett's text.

Replacing it in his pocket, Will wheeled around dramatically—a move that, given its obvious stagecraft and his pint-sized stature, could sometimes also induce jurors to smile; but always, he knew, in sympathy. "None!" He announced, pointing. "Not one of her students has gone on to either of those companies."

"I don't care!" she insisted with hatred. "She's my daughter! She's a *prodigy*!"

"I understand," Will said sympathetically.

"And Dr. Sussman of the Hospital for Special Surgery says she can never put all her weight on that foot again! She can never dance on her toes!"

Will paused, thinking she might cry. "Your Honor....."

"Mr. Tripp," she replied dryly.

"If it please the court, my co-counsel will continue with this witness."

"Without objection?"

"No problem," agreed his opposite number.

"Just one moment."

Will retreated to the defense table. Placing an encouraging hand on his client's shoulder, he whispered in his colleague's ear and stepped aside.

Using the controls on her chair, Marjorie Spivak backed away from the defense table and swung around into open court. On the stand, the witness watched in horrified curiosity as she halted the chair, shut it down and pulled herself unsteadily to her feet. She wobbled a moment; then, with supreme effort, lurched a couple of steps forward. "Now, then, Mrs. Moses," she began, "I know we all sympathize with Katie's injury...."

In the back of the courtroom now, Will decided to linger a few moments longer. Marjorie had been a terrific hire. She was a mediocre lawyer, inarticulate and often slow to grasp the obvious, but she was one helluva cripple.

"The question," she was saying, "isn't whether that wonderful girl will be able to dance the waltz or the tango or...." She stopped, groping for the word. "Or the lambada, if I'm saying it right. At issue is whether she'd have been a *good* ballerina." With difficulty she turned to the judge. "Your honor...."

The judge nodded sympathetically.

"Your Honor," she began again, rocking unsteadily. "Your Honor, with the court's persuasion—pardon me, *permission*—can I enter into the record a video of a recital held at the Waring studio last December?"

"Yes, of course," ruled the judge without hesitation.

Will watched less than thirty seconds of the video, a dozen eleven year olds in tutus dancing to "Waltz of the Flowers," their faces pixilated out to protect them from—Who? What? Child molesters without standards? Dance critics? Katie Moses was the one in pink, no less clumsy than the rest, but quite a bit chubbier, the sort of body that had as much chance of growing into a professional ballerina's as he had of playing offensive left tackle for his beloved Jets.

Katie's mother, oblivious that her case was disappearing down the drain, was beaming. Even left to her own devices, Marjorie couldn't blow this one. Will turned and hurried for the parking lot.

* * * * *

Will seldom visited Bennett at work. Why would he? His brother was so content teaching at Chester College he could scarcely imagine spending his life anywhere else, but having to endure even an hour at the place left Will with the sense of foreboding of a wrongly convicted man hearing the cell door clang shut behind him.

Chester was an *elite college*, which to Will's way of thinking meant it was one of the citadels of The Enemy, its faculty lounges packed with the angry and self-righteous, forever proclaiming their superiority over the rest of us and concocting ways to screw up the world as badly as their own lives already were.

Now, easing into a spot outside the visitor's center, he cut the engine and looked around. Nestled in the Catskills just off Route 27, the place was pretty, no question about that. Hell, with its Greco-Roman Revival buildings half-covered with English ivy and shady lanes of majestic oak, it was a Hollywood fairy tale campus, the ideal setting for, in roughly equal parts, general good times and serious academic inquiry.

In fact, Chester had once been such a place. As a high school history buff growing up forty miles away in the working class town of Catskill, New York, Will had once hoped to go here himself, and actually applied for early admission. Even now he remained something of a sentimentalist—easily crying at movies, especially those where good finally triumphs or hard-hearted father figures go soft in the last reel—but his early experience with Chester College spelled the beginning of the end of his naiveté about the way the world really works. Having never allowed his disability to define him, he failed to so much as mention it on the application, then compounded the mistake by innocently checking the boxes for *White* and *Male*. He was summarily rejected, ending up at SUNY Binghamton instead.

His brother, for once, profited from Will's experience. Applying four years later, he wrote *his* admissions essay on the joys and trials of having a dwarf for a brother, for good measure throwing in something about their working class origins, and he got in, no questions asked. With time off for grad school and work on his PhD. Bennett had been loitering about Chester's 625 verdant acres ever since.

In a real way, their respective views of Chester College had come to represent the brothers' diametrically opposed visions of what truly mattered in this life. Both greatly valued family—that was apparent in their strong mutual devotion—and even after two failed marriages, Will had every expectation of eventually following his parents' sterling example. In fact, living in a Spartan one-bedroom apartment two blocks from his Yonkers office, his one indulgence was on-line dating sites. He was signed up with nine, from zoosk and chemistry.com to jdate and christianmingle, and though he rarely had time to so much as check any of them out, simply knowing that he was out there, in profile, was deeply reassuring, the crucial first step on the road to re-marriage to the right woman and raising several bright, aware, fair-minded, not-easily-duped children. At his knee, they would learn the lessons of history and always speak up when confronted with injustice or rank idiocy, even if it came packaged as compassion or sensitivity. Above all, they would cherish freedom of thought—and none would even consider attending a college where enforced conformity was the rule.

Bennett, on the other hand, insisted that he just wanted his daughter, Casey, to be "happy," which meant, not that he bothered to think it through, fitting in, not causing waves, attending the right college—i.e., one like Chester—which would lead to the right job.

Bennett steadfastly insisted that their parents would have been with him. And it was true that their father, the maintenance manager at the now-defunct Kanfer's resort in the Catskills, and their mother, who worked there part-time as a secretary, were delighted that both their sons were college graduates. Still, they kept up with the times and closely read their sons' alumni magazines, and well before he and his wife died in a collision with a snow plow, George Tripp would remark acidly on the seemingly endless parade of "braying jackasses" who held sway on the nation's campuses. And, of course, since then things had only gotten worse.

Not that Will ever stopped working on his brother. When visiting Bennett's home, he sometimes took unkind pleasure in picking up the course catalogue to chart Chester's downward trajectory. For over a decade, American history majors had no longer been required to study the Revolution or the Civil War—they could skip straight from the oppression of Indians and blacks to the oppression of women and gays. And where once the English Department had boasted renowned teachers of Shakespeare and Milton, now its most popular class was "Deconstructing Gender Roles in the TV Sitcom." Watching his brother squirm as he leafed through the offerings, Will liked to wonder aloud which was his favorite entry. Was it the Environmental Studies class "The Rat as Conservation Guru," the joint English-Women's Studies class "The Clitoris in Modern Fiction," or perhaps "Adultery and Personal Liberation," a requirement for a degree in Modern Religion?

Bennett always countered that, as an associate professor of physics with a specialty in Non-Linear Dynamics and Chaos, what was happening in the liberal arts didn't affect him. If, as Will insisted, the contemporary campus "stunk like the men's room at Grand Central," it wasn't his problem. Like so many scientists, he basically lived for his work—which is to say, primarily in his own head. Though Will wasn't exactly sure what his brother did and sometimes wondered aloud how much of it was real and how much was just hi-falutin' academic horseshit, deriding his field as "geek studies," he couldn't help but respect Bennett's quiet intellectual rigor. Bennett's indifference to the real world could actually be sort of touching. How many other guys he knew would've failed to be suspicious if their wives spent every free moment with a tattooed dyke barkeep?

For all the changes Chester College had undergone in recent years, the school was highly rated as ever, routinely placing among the top five small liberal arts colleges in the annuals devoted to such things. (And why not, since all the others had gone swirling down the toilet with equal abandon?) Which is to say, ambitious parents still competed fiercely for the privilege of doling out exorbitant sums to deliver their unformed progeny to its tender mercies. After all, as Chester proclaimed in its own catalogue, *Chester shapes the young people who make the future.*

That is precisely what Will was afraid of.

Getting out of the car, he made his way toward the quad. As always, he was aware that his very presence presented a quandary for passing students who, while keenly aware of the need to be *sensitive*, especially to those *differently abled*, could not help but stare at the little man with the briefcase in the custom-made boys' size-eight three-piece suit striding their way. Since most averted their gaze as they drew close, Will made a point of trying to catch their attention at a distance. Lithe young women who would otherwise scowl at a man Will's age with the effrontery to blatantly assess their assets, if not seek to have him arrested, only smiled sheepishly in passing. Even the stringy haired young man whom Will accosted, having aroused his particular contempt, sought only to please.

"Nice duds," he remarked, guessing the kid was probably majoring in grievance studies of some kind.

The kid paused, gazing down at his Army jacket and the tie-dyed shirt with the peace symbol. "Yeah," he answered uncertainly.

"Yeah, *Sir*," Will said sharply. "You're in *uniform*, Boy!"

The kid had some idea he was being mocked, and though there was a flash of hostility in his look, he was taking no chances. "Sir," he repeated, continuing on, and Will felt a little better about things.

But only for a moment, for he made the mistake of stopping to peruse the bulletin board at the center of the quad. Among postings for craft fairs, poetry slams, vegan restaurants and free STD clinics were notices for every lunatic cause on campus. *COCKROACH MOMS LOVE THEIR BABIES TOO!* proclaimed one animal rights leaflet, noting *how much we could learn from these precious beings. Yet we slaughter on sight, using poisons developed during earlier Holocausts! OUTLAW PROFIT*

NOW! demanded another leaflet, insisting that *getting WHATEVER we want and need, FREE OF CHARGE, must be recognized as a BASIC HUMAN RIGHT!* But one especially caught his attention, featuring as it did a drawing of two women in fancy early Nineteenth Century dress yoked alongside a pair of black slaves in rags, the four of them straining to pull a wagon driven by a snarling, whip-bearing white man. Above it screamed the words *JANE AUSTEN, WOMAN HATER: A MANIFESTO.*

It was fairly long, so Will snatched it down and retreated to a nearby bench to study it at his leisure. Although he had never actually read any of Austen's stuff, he'd once been induced by a woman on whom he had a serious crush to see one of her movies, which turned out to be all about who's-gonna-marry-whom and guess-which-rich-guy's-the-hero. Old fashioned innocent stuff. But not to the author of the *manifesto*. Firing up a Don Pepin Garcia Black, Will found Austen compared in the very first paragraph to such *recognized literary rapists as Hemingway, Jack London and Kerouac; a worshipper of penis privilege who victimizes her sisters as those brutes never could.* Going into the particulars, it cited Austen's *exaltation of bondage/marriage* and her *denigration of single motherhood* and *other medieval attitudes that even today undermine self-love among young persons of vagina*. Finally came the call to action:

> Here at Chester, we have moved to strike pornography from our classrooms and library shelves. We have declared unfit for student consumption books advocating racism, environmental destruction, bullying and the

> ownership of firearms. We have banished the phallo-supremacist Hemingway and the melanin-phobic Twain. Now, today, recognizing the threat that hetero-normative fascist so-called 'literature' poses to the mental health and safety of us all, let Chester College further affirm our commitment to human values by declaring ourselves the first college in the nation to remove Jane Austen from our shelves!

With a sigh, Will folded the page and stuck it in his pocket. Glancing up, he spotted three students heading his way, two boys and a girl. The girl was remarkably skinny, and as she drew closer, her blank expression gave way to a scowl as she sniffed cigar smoke in the air. Sensing the likelihood of an unpleasant exchange, Will hopped off the bench to put himself on display. Instantly the girl's hostility melted away.

Though dressed in a $600 suit, Will stuck out his hand, scowled and spoke the magic word. "Homeless."

Quickly reaching into her jeans, the skinny girl handed him a five spot, the boys two bucks apiece. Wordlessly, Will snatched them away. Then, for good measure, he stuck out his hand again. "Differently abled." Without hesitation, each handed him another dollar.

Will expressed no thanks, knowing they understood: As one of society's victims, he'd be crazy *not* to be bitter.

He took another puff of his cigar, blowing the smoke their way, and growled "What're you looking at? Leave me alone!"

* * * * *

Bennett's office was in the spanking new science building, Ames Hall, a hundred million dollar state-of-the-art facility paid for by an alum who'd made his fortune in pharmaceuticals.

"What a fool," Will muttered as he rode the elevator up to the fourth floor, reflecting that the guy would be hooted off campus if he dared show up urging today's students to follow in his footsteps.

Bennett's office door was open, and the instant he spotted Will, he assumed a look his brother had never seen before, something approaching rage. "There you are, you bastard!"

"Nice to see you too, Bro," Will said, caught short.

"Close the damn door, dammit!"

Bennett's use of even mild profanity was so out of character Will couldn't help but smile, but only after he'd turned his back to close the damn door. When he again faced Bennett, his expression showed only sympathetic concern. "Okay, Bennett, what's the problem?"

"What's the problem? You ruined my life, *that's* the problem!"

The charge was one with which Will was familiar, but generally it came from a woman toward the end of a romantic entanglement.

"Okay, fine. What's up?"

Bennett rose from his chair and stalked across the room, and for just an instant, Will thought he might hit him. "I did what you said," he whispered, "used the *exact* words."

"Sorry, I'm not following"

"I called her 'a moral black hole!' Like you said!" he hissed.

"Bennett, I didn't tell you to say it to *her,* I just wanted you to get angry." But even as he said it, he was calculating: *It'll only be of use to Laura's lawyer if....* "She doesn't have it on tape, does she?"

"Shh! Hold it down!" Bennett shot back in a whisper. "It's not Laura, I don't think she even knows."

"Why are we whispering?" asked Will, dropping his voice.

"Just in case." He indicated his office. "I can't be sure."

"Who, then?" asked Will, playing along. "Who'd you say it to?"

"I don't know, all kinds of people." Then, off Will's confused look. "The kid at the liquor store... my neighbor's sister... a black guy on the bus...."

The image of his geeky, grief-stricken brother running around emoting to random strangers was pathetic, no question, but it hardly seemed cause for concern. "But I bet it felt good, didn't it?" Will said gently. In fact, a harmless exhibition of public insanity by the usually buttoned-up Bennett brought on by the loss of his wife and child might even end up proving useful. "I'm proud of you."

"I wish I could take it back," he said miserably.

"Trust me," Will said in his normal voice, reaching up to place a reassuring hand on his shoulder, "those people could care less about your problems—they really don't give a damn."

"I know that!" he whispered. "They're not who I'm worried about!"

"Who then?"

"Francine Grabler! She knows all about it."

It took Will half a beat to place the name. *Of course, the name at the bottom of the Jane Austen manifesto!* "You mean," he said, again *sotto voce*, that crazy teacher of—"

"*Professor,*" Bennett said, even now in thrall to the pretensions of the academy. "Of oppression studies—*distinguished* professor. It got around, what I was saying, and she called me this morning. She was screaming, Will! She called me names. A *hater*! She said there was no place at this school for someone like me."

"Bennett...." Will hesitated, chose his words carefully. "Look, I understand. She's obviously a very angry woman."

Bennett shook his head. "You don't know how it is! She's important! And she's out to destroy me!"

"Oh, c'mon, Bennett. Your problems with Laura have nothing to do with her. Or with Chester College."

"She accused me of *verbal rape!*"

"Bennett...."

"I told her I was sorry," he said, miserable. "I tried to explain what happened, that I've been really upset."

"Jesus, Bennett!" he said, wondering how anyone sharing his DNA could ever have come to this.

"Sixteen years I've been at this school." Bennett buried his head in his hands, and his body began convulsing. "You don't know how it is, Will," he repeated. "You just don't know."

"Stop slobbering, will you!" He paused. "Bennett, listen to me... the woman's a lunatic! I was just reading something she wrote attacking *Jane fucking Austen*!" He smiled to emphasize the ludicrousness of it all.

"You don't know what it's like, Will. You don't know."

"Stop saying that. Of course I do!"

Bennett looked up with moist red eyes. "That manifesto was posted two weeks ago. Jane Austen's already gone."

For once, Will was at a loss. He paused. "All right, fine. I'll go see her and straighten it out."

"You don't mean *now*?" asked Bennett, at once hopeful and terrified.

"I'm here aren't I?" Will turned and started for the door.

"Wait!" Bennett looked at him pleadingly. "Tell her it wasn't me, say it was all your idea."

"Right," snorted Will, "you were only following orders. Like Eichmann."

"Exactly," he said hopefully. "Say *that.*"

* * * * *

Like every good lawyer, Will operated by a sacrosanct rule: Know more about the other guy than the bastard can possibly know about you. Though it was already late afternoon, and he was pressed for time, he made a quick detour into the school library and logged onto Wikipedia.

Francine Grabler

Born: Elizabeth Francine Grabler, April 28, 1958, Richmond, Va.

American writer, academic and social activist. Influential in the self-esteem movement in the 1980s, Grabler has penned a number of best sellers, including *I Am My Own Father, Mother and Best Friend, Narcissism is Not a Four-Letter Word* and *The Romance of Self-Adoration,* and was a founder of the seminal anti-cruelty organization WAVE

(We're All Victims Everywhere). In her recent academic work, she has helped popularize the once widely derided idea that all living things, including single-cell organisms and crops, experience violence as pain. Author of *Pain and Anguish,* considered the definitive text on the subject, she currently holds the Phillip J. Donohue Chair for Advanced Oppression Studies at Chester College, in South Chester, NY.

There were several more paragraphs and he raced through them, pausing only to make a few notes.

Ten minutes later, he was waiting in Grabler's outer office as her young assistant tapped gently on her door.

"Yes?"

The assistant opened the door a crack and stuck in his spikey, peroxide blonde head. "Someone to see you." He dropped his voice. "He's a...."

The rest was silent, and from a lifetime of experience Will figured he'd just mouthed that most loathsome of misnomers: "midget." But no matter, it got him what he wanted.

"Well, what are you waiting for?" she said loudly. "Show him in!"

The photo accompanying Grabler's Internet bio didn't do her justice—she wasn't nearly as hideous as he expected. Yes, her unkempt gray hair had all the sheen of withered straw, and her pallor was roughly that of a corpse. But for all that, her features were surprisingly delicate, and with a little make-up she might have actually once been attractive.

That impression was only confirmed when she rose from behind her desk to greet him.

"Come, relax," she said, extending a hand. "I'm here to help. What's your name?"

"Will," he said softly, taking it, noting that her blue eyes were large and shone with genuine kindness. It was hard to tell for sure about her body, swathed as it was in what he'd come to understand was her trademark garb: a colorful muu muu, worn in solidarity with the exercise-averse community. Yet, to his amazement, he was suddenly aware that under other circumstances and with enough liquor in him, he couldn't entirely discount the possibility he might actually be induced to do her.

"How did you hear about our project, Will?"

Just what he figured she'd assume, that he was another ego-challenged loser desperate to be videotaped telling his tale of woe for her *Survivors Project*.

Will shrugged uncertainly. "Read about it." *Just now, in fact, on Wikipedia.* "I was very touched."

She smiled sympathetically, and he saw her teeth could use a cleaning. "Have the bad people hurt you?"

"Isn't that what they do?"

"You've been bullied?"

"Yes."

"By the big people," she said with certainty.

"Even by some little people." As he said it, he realized this was unnecessarily gilding the lily, and tried to pull back. "But I can handle it. I'm pretty tough."

"I'll bet you are."

"I used to get tossed quite a bit."

She looked quizzical, but before she could seek details her phone sounded—the opening notes of *Hurt* by Nine Inch Nails. She glanced at it, and smiled at Will. "Please excuse me just a moment, Will." She picked up the phone and listened for a moment, then said, "This isn't the best time." Then she listened again as some idiot on the other end launched into a sob story.

Will surveyed the room. The shelves were full of her own books and many others on various aspects of oppression. There were also posters. One depicted polar bears wearing armbands with the Jewish star staring forlornly from behind barbed wire in a concentration camp. Another showed a cop, only instead of a cap he was wearing a KKK hood, and beneath were the words *No tolerance for INTOLERANCE!* But his eye lingered longest on the one showing a fully naked coed. It celebrated Chester's annual "Slutwalk," the point of which was *TO GUARANTEE EVERY WOMAN'S RIGHT TO WEAR ANYTHING (OR NOTHING AT ALL!) ANYTIME, ANYWHERE WITHOUT FEAR OF HARASSMENT!* Will thought, *Yeah, right... tell that to your rapist's jury when the Frederick's of Hollywood outfit you wore to the office Christmas party is introduced into evidence.*

"Forgive me, Will," she said, setting aside the phone. She picked up a pen. "Now, Will, can you tell me your last name?"

He hesitated. "Tripp."

Her eyes suddenly narrowed. "There's someone who teaches here with that name."

"Yes." He smiled warmly. "He's my brother."

Rarely in his two decades of experience had he seen anyone's demeanor change so quickly or so completely. Having already written down his first name, she now slashed a line through it. "Is that why you're here?" she said coldly. "Did he send you?"

"Of course not."

"I don't know if you're aware of your brother's behavior, but it cannot be tolerated. He has violated the school's speech code and he must face the consequences!"

"I'm sure whatever it was, he didn't mean anything by it," Will said, staying in character. "He's had a very hard time lately—he's also a victim."

"No!" she said sharply. "He may have his... qualities, but he is a fully abled white man."

There was clearly no point in arguing. Will just looked inexpressibly sad, as he concocted his baldest faced lie yet. "He's a good person. Even though I'm the older brother, he's always protected me. He's protected me from bullies his whole life."

"I'm sure he has," she replied coolly. "But other people also have to be protected from bullies: bullies like *him*."

Oddly enough, she was arousing in him a grudging respect. It wasn't often one of these ostentatiously sensitive types resisted his bullshit, and most of them ate it up with a spoon. But she was as indifferent to his entreaties for mercy as Robespierre when he sent his best buddies off to the guillotine.

Will looked around the room, buying time, taking in the books and the posters. *Ah, shit*, he decided, and came out with it. "I'm also his lawyer."

Her surprise—and annoyance—were evident in a slight widening of the eyes.

"So let's talk turkey—what does he have to do to get off your shit list?"

Her look was a curious mix of contempt and curiosity. "He needs to show that he's atoned."

"By which you mean?"

"I'd like to talk to him about Alexander Kane."

"Who?"

"Your brother will know... a colleague of his."

"Someone in his department...?"

"Someone living in the Dark Ages, and proud of it." Her malice was deep and obviously personal.

"Still thinks the earth is flat, does he?"

She glared at him. "Something like that."

"Has a real problem with diversity, I bet."

Though she made no reply, it was clear he'd nailed it. Not exactly a lucky guess—battles between firebrands like her and old guard defenders of academic tradition had been roiling campuses around the country for more than a decade.

He tried worming his way back into her good graces. "Hey, I'm betting Bennett is with you on this. He was just remarking the other day that there's not a single transgendered person in any of the sciences here! And where are the *dwarves*, for chrissakes!" Despite himself, he couldn't help smirking just a little when he said it. Not that she was buying anyway.

"Just give him the message, *Will*... if that's really your name."

"Got it." He started for the door, then turned back, smiling sweetly. "I mean, on what basis *do* they hire people at this fucking school, anyway? Merit?"

* * * * *

It took only a quick perusal of the school paper, *The Chestonian*, for Will to get the background on the fierce ill will between Grabler and Kane. The head of the Electrical Engineering faculty, an austere and exacting former Marine, Kane had aroused Grabler's wrath by leading the opposition to a proposed new Oppression

Studies Center, budgeted at north of $100 million and aimed at boosting Chester's—i.e., Grabler's—claim to absolute preeminence in the field.

Needless to say, the general sentiment at the school was with Grabler. As one of the several editorials on the subject in the student paper had it, suspiciously echoing Grabler herself,

> Professor Kane is a throwback to the Dark Ages... By virtue of his own privileged (and, it must be said, violence-prone) background, he is grossly insensitive to the great cause of our time, the need to include at the highest echelons those long denied opportunity on the basis of ethnicity, gender or even substandard ability. He bears watching closely—especially how quickly he moves to bring genuine diversity in his own department—and we at the Chestonian are determined to do so.

This seemed to be the tactic Grabler and her allies were pursuing: replacing the remaining despised traditionalists on the faculty, almost all of them in the hard sciences and math departments, with the squishy sorts who now held total sway within the liberal arts. And she meant to do it by fishing for every bit of useful dirt she could get on her chief antagonist, Alexander Kane.

In his office the next morning, Will considered the available options. There were only two. On the one hand, Grabler had nothing in particular against Bennett, whom she clearly regarded as a cipher, so she would let him off easy if he played ball and publicly distanced himself from Kane. But since that would be tantamount to surrendering his soul, Will would never allow it (even if, as he strongly suspected, his brother would). So that left only option two.

Leaning back in his chair, he lit a cigar, drawing in the smoke, his gaze settling on a vintage portrait of the 19th century pornographer and civil libertarian Henry Spencer Ashbee. No doubt about it, the woman was a nightmare. Still, although taking her on would be a bitch, it would also be a pleasure.

In the adjacent anteroom, the player piano suddenly started plinking out "Alexander's Ragtime Band," announcing the arrival of a visitor to the office. Getting to his feet, Will opened the door and looked up at a bearded guy in a rumpled suit, frowning at the piano's dancing keys.

The visitor said, "If you're not gonna keep this thing in tune, I'll take it back!"

"Go ahead," Will replied, grinning. "Never should've taken it in the first place—this is a serious law office, not a damn honky-tonk!"

At her desk across the room, Olga, the Russian-born receptionist, looked distressed. "Please, Mr. Katz, he not mean it. We love player piano." Though ordinarily lacking in both humor and irony, it was Olga who'd come up with the idea of rigging the thing up to start playing whenever anyone came through the door.

"The KGB weighs in," Will said dryly. "Fine, then, we'll keep it—at least until you come up with a baby grand."

"Don't hold your breath, Shorty," Marty Katz replied. "It's not like the Apartments of the Dead give you a selection."

In fact, Katz, a New York city landlord, was responsible for much of the décor that lent the law office of Will Tripp & Associates its distinctive, funky, hand-me-down look, from the Depression-era desks and battered oak file cabinets to the vintage posters for Marilyn Chambers movies and '50s swimwear on the walls; not to mention, occupying a place of honor near the entrance, the gleaming titanium wheelchair that Margaret liked to use for especially important court appearances. These were among the many items constituting the bounty retrieved from the abodes of Katz's deceased tenants.

Katz was not only Will's most reliable client, but one of his closest friends. Will appreciated in a way few others did that Katz's often bawdy good humor masked deep sensitivity. He even wrote poetry—poems that didn't rhyme, so Will knew they had to be good—revealing his melancholy, for this thoroughly decent man was trapped, forever defined by his despised profession. No matter how scrupulously honorable he was in his treatment of others, to the self-righteous he would always be seen as heartless and venal, a mere half-notch in the low-life scale above rapists and murderers. And operating in and around New York only made it worse. Daily, he found himself on the receiving end of some new hell. Every day brought another harassing phone call from some useless government bureaucrat or two-bit PC enforcer, or at best a pricey summons for a plastic bottle allegedly found in a recycling bin intended for metal cans. Each flip of the calendar page was likely to bring word that another of the morally pure was refusing to pay that month's rent as an act of conscience, and he'd long since stopped counting the number of rich scumbags living in Paris or Gstaad who'd earnestly swear in court that they in fact resided in the absurdly under-priced, rent-controlled apartment once occupied by immigrant grandparents. And various judges and city functionaries would not only let them all get away with it, but give Katz a tongue lashing if he dared protest. And there was nothing Katz could do but take it.

"Heh, heh, heh," as he'd observe of his lot in life, twirling a pretend Snidely Whiplash moustache, "I'm the *landlord!"*

But there were also cases—quite a few, in fact—that he couldn't simply shrug off with resignation and gallows humor, those that involved an especially brutal screwing at the hands of a smarmy tenant or a municipal thug. That's where Will came in. Katz soon learned that his new dwarf attorney fully shared his abiding contempt for the enemy, and that he was ready to go to almost any length to bring the bastards down.

The case that first brought them together involved a young woman of Armenian extraction who lived in one of Marty's several buildings on the city's Upper West Side. One busy afternoon, the landlord received a panicky call from the building's super, a Turk, alerting him to the fact that he was en route to the hospital and that the building was swarming with cops. It seemed that a tenant of Armenian descent, claiming the sight of the Turkish super had induced flashbacks to the Armenian genocide of 1915, had come at him with a pair of scissors. At the time, Katz was still represented by someone else, with the result that a housing court judge, after listening to the tenant's tale with deep sympathy, awarded her five years free rent for pain and suffering. Defeated and despondent, Katz retreated to his suburban home and produced an epic poem entitled "Armenian Genocide at 492 Riverside." But he also placed a call to Will Tripp who, using all his wiles and calling in all his chits, had a municipal referee reduce the judgment to a mere six months of free rent. In the world of Marty Katz, that constituted an historic victory.

The case that brought Katz to Will's office today had been ongoing more than two years. It involved a doorman he'd fired after the guy repeatedly failed to show up for work and, on the random occasions when he had, was given to cursing out tenants, especially children. The doorman sued for discrimination, claiming he had in his past a thimble-full of Pequot Indian blood, and the city's Civil Rights Commission found in his favor, determining that he suffered from alcohol addiction, and was thus entitled to a long stretch in rehab at Katz's expense. Once he was deemed cured, Marty was obliged to take him back. When the same thing happened again, Katz went back to the commission, this time with a video documenting the doorman's behavior—and got slapped with an additional fine for harassment. But now the case had taken a dispiriting new turn: the building's tenants association was suing Katz for keeping in his employ the drunk in livery who regularly cursed them out at the door.

"Unbelievable!" Katz exclaimed. "This, after I had an Apartment of the Dead flat-screen TV put in the laundry room!"

Will glanced at the notes he'd made earlier on a scratch pad. "The tenants are mainly white, right?"

"Yeah. So?"

"And there are—what?—twice as many men as women party to the suit."

Katz looked at him quizzically. "I suppose."

"I'm thinking we should maybe turn the tables." He paused. "We'll side with the doorman."

"What?"

"He's a redskin, right? Can he help it if he likes his firewater? Why won't these selfish, angry white men cut him some slack?"

Katz considered a moment, starting to like the sound of it. "Hell, his people never even touched the stuff 'til the white man forced it down their gullets!"

"For once, we'll be the ones pulling the shameless woe-is-me crap and let the other side try to argue it on the merits!" Will paused, relishing the prospect. "Hell, we'll get the Indian to testify for *us*! And if they get incensed and want to fight it, fine—*we'll* drag it out and make those tenants of yours pay their bloodsucking lawyer up the wazoo."

Katz nodded. "It all sounds good... but y'know—"

"What?"

"I just have the feeling that somehow, one way or another, it'll backfire and I'll end up taking it up the ass." He paused. "At the least, we're still gonna be stuck with the fucking Indian. In fact, more than ever."

"I already thought of that." Will placed a comforting hand on his friend's elbow. "I'm guessing those tenants are gonna give us all kinds of new dirt about the guy to work with, stuff he's said and done to their precious little kids. I got a contact at Child Protective Services. Our next move will be to go after him for child abuse."

"Really?"

"If we're lucky, maybe even child *molestation*." Will nodded meaningfully. "Not to worry—*your* bloodsucking lawyer's got your back, ass included."

Katz allowed himself a smile. "I swear, Will, what would you and this penny ante firm of yours do without my business?"

"No problem—chase the ambulance chasers. There are more than enough decent doctors on the receiving end of their bullshit lawsuits. The question is, what would you do without *me*?"

"No argument." With a laugh, Katz rose to his feet and stuck out his hand.

At that moment, he spotted the college catalogue that Will had placed strategically on his desk, facing his way. "Chester College!" he exclaimed in revulsion. "I *hate* that fucking place!"

"I remember."

"Their commie crap totally turned Sarah against me." He paused. "Well, that and her mother."

"I got a case coming up involving Chester. Looks like it could get pretty ugly. I thought you might have some interest."

"Say no more. I'm in!" Katz sat back down. "Okay, I want every detail!"

* * * * *

Warren Frank, president of Chester College, made a steeple of his long fingers and offered his visitors a smile. Facing him across his desk, neither of them smiled back. Each had dressed carefully for the occasion. Alexander Kane, Professor of Electrical Engineering, was wearing a sober grey suit, an American flag pin in the lapel, and a subdued tie; Francine Grabler, sitting just a few feet away yet refusing to acknowledge his presence, was defiant in a baggy sweatshirt and jeans rather than her customary muu muu. Her purpose was to leave utterly no doubt that she was attending this meeting only under what she considered extreme duress.

President Frank looked from one to the other. "Why don't we just sit here for a little while and let the silence wash over us? I find silence can be healing, don't you?"

Frank was big on healing. He used the word often, both in his official role and in daily conversation. Healing was, in his view, central to the mission of the contemporary educational institution. Healing society by pushing for the eradication of social inequity. Healing students by liberating them from the benighted beliefs and values inculcated by unenlightened elders. Healing the earth itself. He defined himself proudly by these beliefs and was not shy about letting others know it.

He'd come to Chester College from the University of California's San Diego campus, after a brilliant teaching career in the cutting-edge field of studies known as Histexuality, wherein long-past historical events are reexamined via speculative research on the sexual behavior and erotic fantasies of key participants. His major work—*Impotence: James Buchanan in Bed and in Office*—not only won the National Book Award, but in arguing that the fifteenth president was paralyzed by the terror of being revealed to an intolerant public as a cross-dressing gay, altered the general view on the origins of the Civil War.

"Good," he said after allowing thirty seconds to pass. "I think that helped, don't you?"

Neither of the others replied.

"Now, we all know why we're here. What we seek is resolution. Healing. We are all part of this wonderful community, and I hope and expect we will leave this room shaking hands and making up."

The Arkansas-born Kane, by nature combative and plain spoken, had promised himself that he would not say anything here that might be taken as antagonistic. It wasn't easy for him. Though his expression remained placid, he was aware of his ears turning a violent red. Bullshit tended to have that effect on him.

For her part, Grabler looked grim, her eyes flashing defiance.

President Frank appeared not to notice, taking their quiescence as assent. Now he turned around the framed quotation he kept on his desk so the others could read it: *The exercise of tolerance is fundamental to modern life. We must all learn inclusiveness and civility.—Warren Frank.*

Kane's eyes widened with incredulity, and he almost burst out laughing as a single word leapt to mind: jackass!

But Grabler nodded vehemently. "Exactly right," she said. "And also kindness."

"Yes," Frank said, pleased. "And that's why we're here." He turned the quotation back toward himself and studied it a moment.

"I also agree," Kane spoke up for the first time. "Agree with it completely." He paused a half-beat, actually managing a smile. Though he spoke in a rumbling Southern growl of a voice and was used to being underestimated, he was a student of history and Shakespeare, and at times like this, he didn't mind showing it off. "To paraphrase Voltaire, think how you want, but let others enjoy the privilege also." He turned to Grabler. "That's all I want for our department. Tolerance. So we can do things the right way, the way they should be done."

"He means the old boys' way," spat back Grabler to Frank. "Hiring and promoting without looking at a candidate's struggles, her demons, the ways she and her forebears have been victimized."

"Goddamn right!" snapped Kane. "I will not have you wrecking my department!"

"Right!" She sneered. "You're all for so-called *qualifications*, the ones designed to exclude!"

President Frank said, "I think perhaps a brief healing silence might be—"

"I don't give a good goddamn about color or gender, but I will not subject my kids to piss-ant instructors with chips on their shoulders who don't know a Discrete Fourier Transformer from a Digital Resistor!"

Grabler stared at him with loathing. But since his anger was making him even more Southern-sounding—which is to say, bigoted—she was inwardly pleased. "Well," she said to Frank, with exaggerated calm, "we're getting some idea of his notion of inclusion, aren't we? And you know what's worse? The students around him start thinking the same way."

"What? I don't for a second...."

"That's what he does. He uses the privilege of teaching at Chester to preach bullying and hatred!"

Kane started to respond, but Frank held up his hand to stop him. "Is that true?" he asked gravely. "Because we can't have that at this school."

"Last week he actually sent a goon in to warn me off," interjected Grabler. "The lawyer brother of one of his so-called colleagues." She turned to Kane, glaring. "But I will *not* be deterred!"

"What are you talking about?" demanded Kane, incredulous. "Who?"

"Bennett Tripp."

"From the Physics Department? I hardly know the man!"

"I'm sure," she said contemptuously. She turned back to Frank. "I have evidence that Bennett Tripp recently committed verbal rape! Right here on campus. And when this brother of his became aware I had such evidence, he came to see me under false pretenses, posing as a legitimate victim!"

"I have no idea what you're talking about!" Kane said, sputtering with rage, his entire face crimson. *"Verbal rape?* What the hell is that, anyway? What, the guy does it with his tongue?" Seeing Frank's shocked look, he knew he'd gone too far, but he was all but beyond caring. "You are a damn menace, Missy! What you need is a good paddling, and I've a good mind to give you one!"

He got to his feet. "I've got students to teach!" he said, and stalked out.

Grabler sat there a long moment, letting the silence work its magic. "You heard it. He threatened me," she said with cool finality. "And something had better be done about it!"

* * * * *

The knock on Will's office door—so diffident as to be barely audible—identified the person on the other side as definitively as a set of fingerprints.

"Come in, Arthur," he called—and, when the head, but not the body, appeared, he added: "*In.* All the way. And how many times do I have to tell you, you don't *have* to knock!"

"I'm sorry, Sir," said Arthur XXX Perkins, entering only a couple of feet into the office.

"Stop apologizing, for chrissakes! And don't call me *sir.*"

"I'm sorry, S—" Only by an effort of will had he avoided tacking on the offending word.

Arthur's manner could hardly have been more at odds with his physical appearance. At 26, a strapping six-foot two, seriously muscled and jet black, he could've passed for a linebacker in the NFL. Little wonder that on dark nights, people tended to drift to the other side of the street at his approach, and not only in dicey neighborhoods but even more so on Manhattan's Upper West Side, where he now lived.

Not that Arthur cared. Adopted as an infant by an upstate New York couple named Pagnozzi, he grew up as a curling aficionado and got his JD degree at the Fairfield Law Center, located in a mall outside Binghamton. On his own time, he dressed in soft cardigans, chinos and penny loafers, and his musical preferences ran from hillbilly rock to the easy listening of Mantovani.

In brief, not only didn't he *feel* black, he was completely indifferent to the sneers of "Uncle Tom" and "Oreo" that sometimes came his way. Soft spoken, even tempered and reflexively civil, he was nothing if not comfortable in his skin, and a bit baffled as to why anyone might think he should be anything else.

Always a respecter of independence of mind, Will had hired him the day they met. Why not? Arthur seemed smart and able, and he loved that he'd already turned down the chance to work for far bigger bucks at several prestigious firms that only wanted him for the color of his skin.

Of course, Will also wanted him for the color of his skin, though not in precisely the same way. If Arthur was to be of maximum use, he would need him sometimes to appear surly, easily offended, and menacing; he would have to intimidate milquetoast lawyers on the other side, for instance, and at least occasionally be able to pull a modified Sharptonesque number on white juries.

It was clear from the start this would take some doing, but Will hadn't anticipated how tough it would be. Arthur was certainly willing enough—in fact, he'd readily accepted the legal name change from Pagnozzi to the blacker Perkins, with the scary XXX in the middle—but aggression was simply alien to his nature.

"Never mind," Will said, muting his frustration. "Let's hear what you've got."

Like Will's other associate, Marjorie, Arthur generally worked from home. He was here today because Will had assigned him the task of enlisting Katz's miserable doorman in the fight against his miserable tenants.

"Well, I found the fellow," reported Arthur.

Will nodded, thinking that probably wasn't hard, since he worked at Katz's building on East 52nd Street; then realized that he rarely actually showed up at the job. "How?"

"PeopleFind, on the Internet."

"Good. Okay. So?"

"You think I should approach him?"

"Yes, Arthur, that's the general idea. I thought you already had."

"He might be suspicious."

"No shit, Kimosabe."

"Larry Harris—doesn't sound to me like he's even a real Indian."

"I'm thinking there's a bonus coming your way if you can prove that."

"He's even less Indian than I am black."

"You're *completely* black, Arthur," Will reminded him

Arthur slapped his forehead. "I know, I know, I'm sorry. Of course I am. I know."

"Say it with conviction, dammit!"

"I'm black and I'm proud," he dutifully replied, undermining the sentiment with a self-conscious grin.

Will sighed. "Anything else, Arthur?"

The phone rang and Will reached for it.

"No, Sir," he said, edging toward the door. "I mean, no, Mr.... Will."

"Good. Now go do a number on that phony Indian."

Will picked up the phone, as behind him the door clicked silently shut. "Yes."

"Will Tripp?"

"Who's this?"

"Barbara Ann Doyle. We should talk."

It took an instant for him to place the name. The bitch who stole Laura from Bennett. "Oh, yeah? Why's that?"

"Cause we've got something in common—that pain in the ass brother of yours...."

"And his whore wife...."

She surprised him with a throaty laugh. "I was about to say that... something along those lines, anyway."

That caught Will short; he couldn't help but be impressed.

"What are you scared of, little man?"

"Just snakes and evil women, and you're both."

"Right. I heard you were the one with balls." She laughed again. "No shit, Tripp, you care about Bennett, you'd best be in my place tomorrow."

* * * * *

"Are you just a brood mare? Is that why you are on this earth—to gratify the base instincts of the lesser sex and then spend the rest of your days trying to survive the consequences, the squalling, loud, sleep-depriving, insanity-inducing consequences, while he, the perpetrator, walks away scot-free?

"We pretend we're long past questions like these, that we're free of the old ways, but no. Look at the messages that barrage our precious, precious girls from our TV and movie screens. Look at the toys in shop windows and the advertisements in magazines that peddle the *universal him's* idea of goodness and beauty. Yes, the *universal him*, who would make us ashamed of the best in ourselves, even as he seeks to drag us back-back-back and down-down-down, denying us the *self*-adoration that is our natural due."

Francine Grabler paused, looking up from the open book she was reading to survey her audience. Of the couple of hundred people arrayed before the podium on folding chairs in Washington D.C.'s legendary Politics and Prose book store, a good eighty percent were women. Some could have been her students, but the vast majority were far older; veterans, as she was, of the revolution that had so dramatically transformed American life, and still justifiably furious, as she was, about how much remained to be done and that there were so many out there forever plotting to return things to the way they used to be. From the very beginning these women had been the core of her reading public, and she could count this evening on some of them buying three or four books.

But of course, her words were mainly directed to a far larger audience, the one that would be seeing her in coming weeks on C-Span, thanks to the camera inconspicuously recording the event in the back. As an aid to viewers, a conscientious publicist had set up adjacent to the podium a poster for *The Romance of Self-Adoration.* It showed the book's cover—an obese nude caressing herself with the multiple arms of an Indian goddess—as well as the publisher's email.

Wary by nature and experience, in public settings like this, Grabler was often jumpy. After all, she had enemies, lots of them, and who knew what one of them might try to do? Younger men in particular spooked her. Even at Chester College they occasionally gave her trouble, presuming to challenge ideas that were sacrosanct; of course there were procedures in place to deal with them. Beyond the college's cloistered confines, their brethren were free to be crudely derisive, and more than a few were menacing in their very presence. It was not for nothing that even for her appearance here tonight, when otherwise in her element, that she had insisted on special security.

She resumed reading. "I see the tragedy unfolding before me every day, for even some of the remarkable young women I teach have been seduced by the *universal him* into the cult of child-adoration. They even speak of it in the propagandist's very words: "natural," "healthy," and most insidious of all, "normal."

"We must cry No! No, no, no, no, no! For first, always, if there is to be freedom and fulfillment and *progress*, there must be *self*-adoration!" She looked up at the audience, and smiled warmly. "Thank you."

The applause was sustained and heartfelt.

Grabler cast a quick glance at a well-dressed black man in the front row, her special guest for the evening, and was reassured to see him smiling and applauding with the rest. He was Milton Morgan, special assistant to the president, and she'd made time earlier on this quick trip down from Chester for a preliminary but very pleasant conversation about a possible appointment to the Department of Education as Under Secretary for Diversity Enforcement if not to the top job itself. Given the situation at Chester, it certainly didn't hurt to have other options.

"I believe Professor Grabler has time for just a few questions," said a store representative, materializing before her. "And then, of course, she'll be available to sign your books."

She pointed. "Yes."

A heavyset woman near the front got to her feet. "First of all, this is such an honor! You are so wise, and have meant so much to me over the years!"

Grabler nodded graciously. "Thank you."

"I'm just wondering, how do you manage it all—the teaching, the writing, the public speaking—and still have enough time and energy for self-adoration? Because after a hard day's work, I can barely drag myself into bed."

"Well, I suggest you buy the book and find out." Grabler laughed with the audience. "No, seriously. It is a matter of passion. And what you will find is the passion you devote to self is returned many-fold in life force."

A dozen arms waved in the crowd, and Grabler pointed at a woman toward the back. "Yes."

"My question is, what can we *do* about all the child adorers out there—bothering us with their spawn in restaurants, unfairly taking time off from work, and—"

"I know." Grabler held up a hand to stop her. "I think we all do." She paused to allow for the appreciative laughter, and in that moment spotted a young man a couple of rows behind the questioner. He was not smiling, but staring at her with a searing intensity that gave her the creeps. It was only by an act of will that she looked away to focus on other, friendlier faces. "Actually, it's really not all that hard," she said, easing into a meme by rote. "You're a victim, and you can't be shy about saying so! Embrace your victimhood! It's always the best response to the evil of patriarchy."

Fifteen minutes later she was sitting at a table, the woman from the store beside her, briskly pulling a book from the stack with the approach of each customer and snapping it open to the title page for her signature. The line snaked to the back of the store, but Grabler's focus was on the young man as he slowly made his way toward her. She thought of alerting security, but Milton Morgan was standing off to the side, watching, and she didn't want to appear weak or foolish.

Finally he was in front of her, and Grabler looked up into a pair of hard grey-brown eyes. She offered a smiled but he didn't return it.

"Who would you like it made out to?" asked the store woman.

"Just a signature," he replied tonelessly. "It's for my collection."

* * * * *

Will hadn't been inside Doyle's place, Seventh Heaven, since his post-toss law school days, back when it was a sawdust-on-the-floor joint going under the name The Pour House and its clientele were workers from the nearby battery factory. These tended to be sullen, understandably so, since it was later established that many suffered from chemical poisoning, and the bar was known as a brawler's haven. But now the factory was long gone, along with most of the other blue collar jobs in this economically depressed region, and the only dining establishments in town that seemed to be thriving were the couple of overpriced chi chi restaurants favored by *New York Times* subscribing Chester College faculty and the shrinks from the South Chester Psychiatric Center.

Yet entering the place, Will was struck by how little it had changed. Same sawdust. Same heavy oak tables with candles in old wine bottles. Same jukebox in the corner, playing Elvis, Sinatra and Nat King Cole.

"I thought about changing the music," said Barbara Ann Doyle, facing Will across a table in back, "but then I thought, nah, give the little bastards an education." She laughed and jerked her head vaguely in the direction of the college. "God knows they're not getting much of one over there."

No getting around it, Will liked her. All right, she was pretty rough around the edges, kind'a like Charlize Theron at the beginning of that movie about the dyke serial killer, before she went totally off the rails looks wise, but Will wasn't the sort to hold that against anyone, not when it came with the no bullshit directness of this broad.

"So you don't think much of Chester College," he observed mildly, probing.

"Ah, shit, I take the little bastards' money, else I wouldn't be in business, but otherwise...." She took a long pull from a bottle of Ithaca Dark, the house brew. "Why, do you?"

"Nah, I prefer my lobotomies the old fashioned way, a quick snip to the prefrontal cortex."

She cackled. "Ah, shit, the kids aren't the problem—some fascistic tendencies, but that's not their fault. They don't even begin to know how much they don't know. Hey, I talk to 'em every day."

Will glanced over her shoulder through a haze of cigarette smoke, noted the dozen or so kids at several tables talking animatedly, their eager optimism bespeaking ignorance of both past and present.

"Glad to see you still allow smoking," he observed.

"Allow it? I *encourage* it!"

"Food any better since the last time I was here?"

"What, you some kind'a gourmet or something?" She laughed again and, despite himself, he could definitely see why Laura would prefer her to Bennett. "Better be—turns out the last owner was using horse meat." She raised a hand, scouts' honor. "I shit you not." She paused, raised her beer. "Anyways, they come for this, not the food. Plus, I keep a big bucket of rubbers in both bathrooms, and I got a room in the back with a couple of mattresses, for those that can't wait to get back to the dorm." She smiled. "See, in some ways I do keep up with the times."

Will waited a moment. "Okay. So what's this big news about my brother that couldn't wait?"

"No offense, but he seems like a total loser."

"None taken."

"What is it about that guy, anyway?"

"Don't ask." He shook his head. "But I promised our parents I'd always watch out for him." He sipped his beer. "Dumbest fucking promise I ever made."

"Did you know he calls the house five or six times a night?"

This was new information, but Will's sharp nod suggested otherwise. "What can I tell you? He's hurting."

"Whining, crying. What's worse, she listens to him and whimpers back. I'm getting to where I can't take it. They're a pair of infants, the two of them."

"So drop her, send her back to him. End of problem."

"No, no, no," she said, waving this away. "Other than that...." She hesitated. "Damn my sorry soul, I truly like the woman... might even love her."

Will's expression was unchanged. "What, the New Age crap doesn't throw you?"

She smiled. "There is that. But you know, I'm one of those for better or worse types."

"Not me."

"Yeah, I wouldn't guess you'd be easy."

"But I know what I like: spirit! Hell, if you were free, I'd get you naked and use those hooters of yours for leverage, if you know what I mean."

"You really are a filthy little gentleman, aren't you?" she said admiringly.

Will cleared his throat. "But of course I'm here today in my capacity as an officer of the court."

Barbara Ann laughed again and took a sip of beer. "Anyway, I'm absolutely crazy about the kid—and, frankly, between you and me, I'm a lot better for her than either of them."

He looked at her evenly and nodded. "I don't doubt it. But I didn't have to rush up here to find out my brother's a dickhead."

"Well, anyway, he's not the one I'm worried about."

He leaned in closer, seizing the table to keep his balance since his feet were a foot off the floor. "What... they're pressuring Laura?"

"Driving her nuts, as if she's not hysterical enough already."

"Francine Grabler," he said, a statement not a question.

"She's behind it of course, but she lets others do the dirty work. They want a statement from her accusing that brother of yours of some pretty nasty stuff."

Will nodded. This was bad news, but hardly a surprise. In fact, deeply skeptical by nature, he was suddenly wondering what side Doyle was really on. "So fine, let Laura put out a statement."

"Excuse me?" she said, caught short.

"She can't do any worse to him than she's done already. She can accuse away. As far as I'm concerned, it's all bullshit anyway. You know it, and I know it. And, know what? I'll fucking destroy her if she tries!"

"She'd *never* do that! And if she wanted to, I'd never let her! Jesus H. Christ! Besides, they're not interested in ripping him publicly. They want to use the statement to blackmail him."

"All right, all right. I just wanted to hear it. So we're good."

"What? You little scumbag, you were *testing* me!" She was trying to sound angry, but he could see she was also amused.

"Exactly, and you pass. No hard feelings."

"Course not, you're just doing your shitty job."

He smiled. "So tell me, how'd someone like you ever turn out to be one of the good guys?"

"Like they say, familiarity breeds contempt. I know these self-righteous oppression types. The women's studies and English departments, a good half of them, I know... *intimately*. And let me tell you, they are scary."

Will nodded. "Okay...."

"They *will* destroy him. They'll get his ass fired, maybe even put him behind bars. Trust me, I've seen it happen before."

Will felt a tightening in the pit of his stomach, but his expression was unchanged. "Well, thanks, appreciate it. And just so you know, we'll work with you to keep Laura out of it...."

"Big news. Like you'd ever want her out there."

He laughed, easing himself down from his chair. "Just saying...."

"Where you going?"

He hesitated. "What do you mean?"

"We could'a had this whole conversation on the telephone—you're here for a reason." She paused. "There's a rally on campus tonight. *Against hate*. At 7:30." She checked her watch. "That gives you roughly twenty-five minutes."

* * * * *

As Will stepped from his car in the parking lot, the rally was already underway. Someone was haranguing the crowd, the voice sounding quavery as a turn-of-the-century recording over the distant loudspeaker. Only when he arrived over the crest of a hill and the makeshift platform came into view was he aware that the reedy voice belonged to a guy who was, minimum, ninety years old. So pitifully thin his jeans threatened to slide down his bony frame, he was held upright by a sturdy student on either side.

"One two three four," he was screeching, long white hair whipping in the wind, "*we don't want your fucking war!*"

The crowd of several hundred seemed momentarily confused, then a couple of voices rose in approval.

"Yeah!"

"Tell it!"

And there was a smattering of applause.

Now, with the aid of one of his helpers, he held his fist aloft, urging the crowd on. "Five, six, seven eight, we don't want *your fucking hate!*"

At this, the crowd screamed their approval, and instantly took up the chant. "No more hate! No more hate!"

"Who *is* that guy?" Will inquired of a girl nearby in a t-shirt with a drawing of a grinning, bare-assed Michael Moore farting in Sarah Palin's face.

The kid looked incredulous, but softened when she saw Will. "Professor Novak—he taught sociology here way back in the '60s. Isn't he great?"

Will flashed a grin meant to be inscrutable.

"He really helped turn the school around," she added.

"Well, out with the old...." Will nodded toward the front, where the old man was being gently urged away from the microphone by his handlers. Only now, summoning all his strength, he lurched back and grabbed it anew. "Drop acid, not bombs!" he screamed, displaying a defiant middle finger.

"All riiiight!" enthused the kid who jumped up to take his place at the microphone, his ponytail bouncing behind. "Professor Novak! A legend! We all gotta climb on his shoulders, people—that's what this is all about! The same way in his time he went after Nixon and Hitler and McCarthy, we gotta nail the haters in our time!" Turning serious, he surveyed the crowd. "You can ask any shrink: Hate is a disease! And it's a million times worse than any STD! It's like clap of the soul, people, and there *ain't no cure*!"

He paused, dropped his voice. "We like to think hate is something that happens only to other people, far away. But that's wrong. In fact, me personally, I never even knew what hate was until I got *here,* to *Chester College*—and found it in another student!" He stopped, let the shocking fact sink it. "This guy, at first he just seemed like another kid in the dorm, you know? It's not like there was a big *H* on his forehead or anything, that's not how it works." He stopped again. "But one night it all came out. A bunch of us were talking, you know, about how, like, the people locked up behind bars in this country, they're only there because they're, like, poor or young or got the wrong color skin, and how that should have us all pissed off all the time!"

From the crowd came a murmur of agreement.

"Like Professor Grabler says, we're all victims, but they're, like, *super-victims!* But this kid, all at once he starts *arguing*, saying lots of them *deserve* it, and it's okay that they're stuck in cages and get fucked up by the cops because they're...." He made quotes with his fingers. "*Criminals.* They've broken the..." more quotes "*law.*"

He stopped to allow the enormity of this outrage to sink in. "It was sickening, literally, but he's saying this garbage like it's totally *okay* and he's got a right to his..." finger quotes "*opinion*, and it was, like, free speech. Except it's *not* free speech! It's *hate* speech! And it's *not* okay! That didn't happen in Iran or Israel. It happened right over there in Browder Hall. And it wasn't some guy in a history book, it was a kid down the hall. "So here's the question each and every one of us has to ask ourselves: if we don't do something about hate and the so-called people that spread it, who will?" He paused, then began to chant. "Stop the hate, stop the hate, stop the hate...."

As the crowd took it up, Francine Grabler slipped behind the mic, striking in a jet black muu muu. Recognizing her, they broke into the loudest applause yet.

She waited, surveying the faces before her with weary sadness, and when she flung up her arms for quiet, Will was reminded of the sorcerer in Disney's *Fantasia*, commanding the waters to recede; in a millisecond, all was silence.

She removed the microphone from the stand and moved several steps to the right, then back again. "Jeff is too modest," she began evenly. "What he neglected to say is that someone *did* do something about that hateful student. *Jeff* did something. He came to me, and we worked together, and as a result, that young man was brought before the Student-Faculty Committee on Civility and Mores. And you'll be happy to hear, he is no longer a student at Chester. So let's all show our appreciation to Jeffrey Hornung."

There were hoots of approval and a sustained round of applause.

"But sadly, Jeff is right," she resumed. "The haters are *still* all around us. And even when we think we have weeded them out or led them to enlightenment, they are *thinking* hate—silently abusing people of color, people of vaginas or people of penises who yearn to be people of vaginas; and so many, many others. Abusing, abusing, abusing! Silently abusing our beloved victims!"

She had them transfixed, and she knew it. Even Will found her delivery oddly mesmerizing.

"Make no mistake," she continued, "our enemies are bold. And why not? Haven't they always been protected? By tradition? By privilege? By the patriarchy? By the police and military that do their bidding?" She paused meaningfully. "And, yes—here at Chester—by tenure!"

This is what the crowd had been waiting for, and the roar of approval that followed lasted twenty seconds, punctuated by attempts to revive the chant. But Grabler raised her arms again to cut it off.

"For, make no mistake, the haters and the bullies are not just in the dorms, but in the faculty lounges and, yes, in the front of classrooms and lecture halls. For too long they have been used to getting their way. And now that they feel threatened, now that you and I are demanding genuine change, they will go to any lengths to stop us. *Any* lengths—yes, including violence! In fact, I must tell you, I was personally threatened by one of them just this week!"

At this, the crowd seemed to gasp as one in horror and incredulity.

Grabler waited a moment, then screamed. "*But we will not be intimidated, will we?*"

"*Noooo!*"

"*This time we will fight back, won't we?*"

"*Yessss!*"

"Yes, we will." Grabler agreed in her normal voice, nodding. She allowed herself a small smile. "I have here a sheet of paper." She held it aloft, so the crowd could see. "It has a name on it, the name of the Chester College faculty member who has sworn violence against me."

"Kane!" someone shouted, provoking a chorus of angry boos.

"But as we know, hate does not grow in a vacuum," she continued. "There are others at this school that give hatred sanction and quarter." Abruptly she brandished another sheet of paper. "And they too, must now decide which side they are on or face the consequences!"

As the crowd again launched into the chant, Will turned and started back toward the parking lot.

"Where you going?" called the girl in the Michael Moore t-shirt. "Stick around, there's gonna be free beer."

"Can't," he called back amiably. "I'm late for a book burning."

"Oh, okay. Have fun!"

* * * * *

Will didn't get back home until almost 2:00 a.m., but at precisely 9:00, he was in his office, lighting the day's first cigar and snatching up the phone.

"President Frank's office."

Will pegged the receptionist to be on the wrong side of middle age, and there was no nonsense in her tone.

"Good morning. My name is Will Tripp. I was wondering if I might have a moment of his time."

"Will he know to what this is in reference?"

To what this is in reference—priceless! "I'm the brother of Bennett Tripp, who's on the Chester faculty." He paused. "I'm also his attorney.

"I see." The way she said it seemed to suggest that she knew Bennett *needed* an attorney—or was that just his imagination? "I'm afraid Dr. Frank is extremely busy."

"I understand that. Of course...." He cleared his throat, threw out his trump card. "I'm also a dwarf."

"You mean a little person?" she said, at once clarifying and correcting.

"Yes," he allowed, and spat out the despised term. "A *little person.*"

"One moment please."

"Mr. Tripp," came the voice seconds later, all easy bonhomie. "Warren Frank."

"Thanks for taking my call."

"No problem."

"I was in Chester last night, and I attended the rally." Silence, so Will pressed on. "You can probably guess why I'm calling."

"Actually, no."

"It seems to me that certain *aspersions* may have been cast involving my brother, Bennett."

"I'm sorry, I don't follow."

"Well, I'd just like your personal assurance that Bennett is under no suspicion of any...."

"Of course not. Dr. Tripp is a valued member of our faculty...."

Will glanced at his vintage mini-recorder to make sure the tape was spinning. *Good old wire taps. Say what you will, they never go outta style.*

"That's good to hear. Because I'm hoping we can get together to discuss this and put an end to this slander once and for all."

"Well, I'm afraid I've got a very tight schedule."

Fucking weasel, Will thought. *Just waiting to gauge which way the wind will blow.*

"I don't know if you've been informed, but I'm a little person."

"Yes, Mr. Tripp, and I am honored to know that. Unfortunately, I cannot discriminate, even on *behalf*, so to speak."

"Of course not."

"Perhaps in several weeks? You can work it out with my assistant...."

"Thank you, I'll do that. That's good of you."

"That's my job, Mr. Tripp, to allay pain and promote healing."

Hanging up, Will leaned back and got maybe a minute and a half of smoking pleasure before resigning himself to the inevitable and punching in his brother's number. Bennett answered after half a ring.

"I was about to call you." His brother sounded surprisingly rational, and it occurred to Will he hadn't yet heard.

"Yeah, well, that's good, 'cause we have to talk."

"Will," he wailed, the façade dissolving, "you've got to help me!"

"I know all about it, and I'm working on it. No need to do anything yet."

"You know about it?" Bennett said, confused. "The petition?"

"Petition?"

"Dr. Kane's written a petition. He's circulating it to the math and the sciences faculty, plus... I don't know, I also hear it's going to some Latin teachers."

"What's it say?"

"I don't know, all kinds of gobbledygook about academic freedom."

Goobledygook? "Listen, Bennett," he replied, keeping his annoyance in check, "are you aware there was a rally last night? And that that bitch Grabler is definitely...." *Is there a less menacing word? Nah, what the hell.* "Targeting certain faculty members."

"Me?"

"How can you sound so surprised? Not just you. Anyone she thinks is on Kane's side."

"But I'm not, Will, you know that! Oh, God!"

The office door opened, revealing Marty Katz. "But I do have some good news," Will said, motioning Katz over. "Laura definitely won't be cooperating with Grabler, so you're clear on that end."

"How do you know?" he said, suddenly hopeful. "Did you talk to her?"

"Never mind how I know. And don't get your hopes up about her coming back anytime soon, 'cause that's not happening."

"She said that?"

"Just focus, goddammit. I need you to tell me more about this petition."

"Oh, God, I don't know, it just says.... Hold on, I'll get it."

Will turned to Katz and shook his head wearily.

"Hey, could be worse. *My* brother's doing twelve to fifteen for ripping off the nuns of the Sisters of Charity."

"You don't have a brother."

"Just trying to make you feel better."

"It's pretty short," Bennett said, back on the line. "At the top it says 'In Defense of Academic Freedom at Chester College.'"

"Okay."

"And then it talks about how Chester has a long tradition of free inquiry...."

"Bullshit, but you gotta say it."

Will switched the phone to speaker so his friend could listen in.

"And how important that has always been to the education kids get here....."

"Okay."

"And how that's now under threat from—this is a quote—'agenda-driven zealots, on campus and off.'"

Katz whistled approvingly.

"Um hmm," Will said. "Then what?"

"Then there are three demands, a sentence each: that the administration reaffirm Chester's commitment to intellectual diversity; that they stand behind any faculty member under attack on ideological grounds; and that all hiring decisions at Chester be made strictly on the basis of merit, so—I'm quoting here—'to get the very best people in every field, the liberal arts included, regardless of race, gender, ethnicity or political orientation.'"

"Jesus, talk about going straight for Grabler's jugular!"

"So you don't think I should sign it, right?"

"You goddamn well better!"

"Please, Will." He paused. "Could I sign anonymously?"

"Right, there's an idea."

"So you're saying...."

"Listen, Bennett," he cut him off, "I'm not your conscience, do what you gotta do. I got someone here, we'll talk later."

"Wait, Will. I just—"

Hanging up, Will turned to his friend with resignation.

"I don't envy you," Katz said. "That guy's worse than any brother I could ever dream up."

* * * * *

"Okay," Marty Katz said half an hour later. "Just tell me how much this is gonna cost me."

"You can't put a price on freedom of thought, Marty, you know that. Or justice." Will grinned. "No way to know until we know, right Danny?"

Across the table, Danny Valenzuela had been studying a photo of Francine Grabler, so he missed the exchange. "Sorry?"

"Mr. Katz was wondering about the cost of your services."

"I'd almost do this one for expenses," Danny said, then caught Katz's eye and smiled. *"Almost."*

Will was pleased that both Katz and Valenzuela, having gotten a quick overview, seemed as passionate about the case as he was, but he wasn't surprised. The three of them had worked together before—Will the lawyer, Katz his landlord client, Valenzuela the private investigator charged with exposing the phony claims of deadbeat tenants—and he knew what they were made of. Within minutes of Valenzuela's joining them in the office, as he recounted what Grabler and her allies were trying to pull up at Chester College, he could already read indignation in both sets of eyes.

Now, down the street, at a back booth in the Euclid Diner, the three of them were discussing the situation over breakfast.

Valenzuela turned the photo toward Katz. "You seen this?"

"Yeah."

"Man, that is one ugly woman. *Una chancha verdad.*"

"I pulled that off the web," Will said. "Believe it or not, she's really not that bad in person."

"Her hair looks like a viper's nest," observed Katz. "Something's *gotta* be living in that thing!" To the landlord, who so despised Chester College based on unhappy personal experience, Grabler seemed the very embodiment of the place.

"Well, yeah, there is that," Will said, reaching for the photo to take another look. He guessed it was a publicity shot, for she'd gone to considerable lengths to obscure any hint of physical attractiveness, lest she offend her natural constituency. "Anyway, trust me, her *mind* is a lot uglier." He turned to Valenzuela. "She's a real *caña.*"

Danny laughed. "You mean *caja*—that's a cunt. A *caña's* a dick. Get it straight."

Catching this, the Hispanic waiter passing by with a coffee pot in each hand suppressed a smile.

"In this case, either works," Will said. "This particular cunt is also a prick."

"Coffee?" asked the waiter.

"Sure, hit me," Will said, indicating his half empty cup.

"Regular or de-caf?"

"No need for that, Jose," Katz said, "they're my friends." He turned to Will. "A specialty of the house—they put the same stuff in both pots. Right Jose?"

Jose gave a little laugh and an embarrassed shrug.

"I approve," Will said, offering his cup. "Always nice to see a healthy contempt for the customer."

Katz knew this, and much else about the Euclid Diner, because he enjoyed a special relationship with the middle-aged Greek owner, Teddy: in exchange for Teddy's occasional use of a basement room in one of his nearby buildings as a love nest, Marty enjoyed unlimited free breakfasts, and so could be found here most every morning.

"So it's not like English?" Will asked. "The two words can't be used interchangeably to basically denote an asshole?"

"No, they can't. Technically they're gender specific." Danny reached into the plate of fries and swirled a couple around in the third of a bottle of ketchup he'd dispensed onto an adjacent plate. "But most people would get your point."

This was one of the ancillary benefits of using Danny as a PI—he offered top-notch instruction in the strategic use of Spanish slurs. Just a couple of months ago, facing a Puerto Rican woman on the stand who spoke in halting English and projected the loving humanity of Mother Theresa as she explained that, no, she absolutely had not *abandoned* her $340 rent-stabilized, three-bedroom apartment on West 95th Street as claimed by her greedy and immoral landlord, Martin Katz; she simply had needed to spend the last two and a half years in South Beach caring for her AIDS-stricken cousin Ramon. As New York juries will in such cases, this one seemed set to ignore the evidence that, in fact, Ramon was neither ill nor her cousin, but a Peruvian drug dealer and her lover; until, that is, Will sidled up beside her and whispered *"Madre de un mentiroso puta zorra"* and, like the flicking of a switch, she erupted in outraged profanity. Even better, it was in English. "Fuck *you*, you little cocksucker!" she screeched, her face hot red. Realizing too late, she turned to the jury and implored, "*Dios mío*! You no hear? He call me whore!"

But Danny Valenzuela's real value was that he was relentless. A "Mexican attack Chihuahua," Katz admiringly called him, for small of stature and possessed of a choir boy's face, his looks inspired in his prey both trust and carelessness, especially in women. If his self-regard could occasionally verge on the insufferable—he considered himself so gifted at artifice and manipulation that he could get even the human equivalent of a stone to start coughing up useful information—it was not without basis. His uncanny ear for language gave him the ability to pass as not only every variety of Hispanic but, when necessary, as a Ukranian or Lithuanian or generic Middle Easterner. Such was his ability to root out dirt on even the most wily and unscrupulous of Katz's tenant-foes that Will and Marty kept him on retainer; notwithstanding the fact that he was only semi-legal, having married an elderly Midwesterner of questionably sound mind on her death bed.

"So how deep you want me to go?" Danny asked, stuffing his face with a new batch of fries.

"As deep as you have to. The woman's a cancer; she's gotta be stopped. On the up side, I think we've got a little time. The college president's such a pussy, I doubt he'll move too fast."

Danny nodded. "So you're saying wherever it takes me—"

"Look under every goddamn rock." Will popped open his briefcase and began unloading its contents. "The woman's almost a blank slate—most of the stuff in her official bios is crap. It's all basically love letters." He riffled through the material. "Here's some of the articles she wrote, and a couple of the books."

"Listen," interjected Katz, "do try to keep the costs within reason."

"Oh, Christ, Marty, this isn't about dollars and cents, we're in a war here! What's the word for *cheapskate*, Danny? *Tacomo*?"

"*Tacaño*. Or *roñica*." He gave Katz an apologetic shrug. "I didn't say it, he did."

"A fuckin' *war*, Marty! 'The summer soldier and the sunshine patriot will, in this crisis, shrink from the service of their country and—'"

"All right, goddammit."

As Will well knew, nothing so readily stirred his friend like Paine's *The Crisis*.

"'But he that stands by it now, deserves the love and thanks of man and woman...'"

"Hear that, Marty, the thanks of *woman*," chimed in Valenzuela.

"And let's face it, where else you gonna get that?"

"Fine," allowed Katz. "All right."

"Don't worry, I'll keep careful accounts. Every penny accounted for."

"Goddamn it, I said all right!" He indicated the material before him. "You read any of this crap?"

"About half a page of this." Will picked up the paperback copy of *I Am My Own Father, Mother and Best Friend*. "I swear, man, I still haven't recovered."

Danny, meanwhile, was studying her bio. "Born in Richmond, Virginia. Wonder if she still has family down there."

"Friends, colleagues, whoever. Especially enemies. You can bet your brown ass she's got plenty of those."

Danny nodded and picked up *Narcissism is Not a Four Letter Word.* Flipping to the introduction, he read aloud. "We live in a time of deceit. A time when the good are crushed by the powerful and are slapped down for even daring to complain. A time when caring for yourself, defending yourself, *loving* yourself is a sin, and inflicting pain is the ultimate virtue."

Danny looked up, an impish look in his innocent eyes. "You're in good hands. I hate her already."

* * * * *

Alexander Kane knew things were bad, but he had no idea they were this bad. Staring down at the petition, he could only shake his head. "Un-goddamn-believable."

The first signature at the bottom of the page was as bold as John Hancock's on the Declaration of Independence: his own. Next came two junior members of his department.

The four that followed were each in a different hand, but otherwise identical: "Anonymous."

He looked up at the pair of students standing uncomfortably before his desk. "Who *are* these pussies?"

"From the Physics Department," replied one of the young men, Sergei, betraying a pronounced Russian accent. "It was only way they would sign."

"Who the hell came up with such an idea?"

Sergei pointed to the first *Anonymous* on the list. "Professor Tripp."

"*That* guy?"

"But still he seem nervous when he sign."

"What a pussy!" He paused. "What about Jack Cronin? 'Cause when I talked to him, he was all gung ho."

Sergei pointed to the third *Anonymous*. "I think they all talk about it together."

"Christ almighty!"

"How 'bout you, Than?" he said, turning to the Vietnamese kid. "No luck with the math folks?"

"A couple told me they'd think about it. Mr. Bowen—I had him in Linear Algebra and Differential Equations. Also Ms. Plank. But when I went back to see them, their offices were closed." He paused, then elaborated. "No one in there."

"Right, I get the picture." Kane snorted. "I've pulled that one myself, but only when it was some asshole I was dodging, not my *responsibility*!"

More than half of Kane's Electrical Engineering majors and almost every one of his top students were foreign-born, but Sergei and Khan stood out above the rest. He loved and respected them as he did his own grown son, now abroad in the military, and not just for their dedication to science. Both were from difficult circumstances—Sergei having immigrated from Russia at fourteen, Khan the son of Vietnamese boat people—and they'd gotten to where they were by virtue of their character. Not only did they share a work ethic and general seriousness about life he almost never saw in their American contemporaries, but they had guts. From the start of this fight both had been so steadfast in their support that he sometimes wondered, with a twinge of guilt, whether they fully grasped the jeopardy in which they were placing themselves.

"Mathematicians." Kane smirked, making light of the disaster at hand. "I've always said they're a royal pain in the rhombus."

The two boys stared at him, expressionless, something not uncommon when Kane veered from the familiar precincts of advanced science. Bright as they were, there were just some cultural gaps that could never be bridged.

"That's another one of my jokes, men—not much of one, I grant you, but times bein' what they are... well, let's keep at it. Let's force every lily-livered one of 'em to put himself on the record, one way or the other. Meanwhile, we'll keep up with the media stuff."

This was Kane's other ongoing effort, trying to bring public attention to the issue via the press. But if anything, it was going even less well than the petition. The release he'd sent out to several hundred papers and broadcast outlets, headed "Academic Freedom Under Siege at Chester College?" was deliberately non-inflammatory—he'd even added the question mark at the last moment—yet the only response had been a couple of passing mentions in insignificant blogs. Even the local *Chester Weekly Independent* had ignored it. Although it occurred to Kane that perhaps another pitched battle between campus activists and traditionalists no longer qualified as news, he also couldn't avoid the suspicion that many journalists, invested in *change*, were simply on the other side; or, at any rate, had no interest in alerting fair-minded readers to the startling influence of people like Francine Grabler on what today passes for higher education.

Kane abruptly stood. "Gentlemen, I thank you for your good work," he said, and he strode out his office door.

The students exchanged a look and hurried after him, without knowing quite why, except that this odd, gruff man was the best teacher they'd ever had, and they felt they'd somehow failed him.

* * * * *

Danny Valenzuela walked slowly up Richmond's West Grace Street, studying the homes lining the broad avenue. An architecture buff, self-taught and passionate, he admired the structures' understated elegance. Constructed in the aftermath of the Civil War, their sweeping slate roofs and white colonnade façades transported him to that other, seemingly simpler time. Though the neighborhood had been through hard times, only rebounding in recent years with gentrification, even those buildings that had not yet been renovated retained a quiet dignity.

This was one of the aspects of the job Danny enjoyed most—the opportunity to experience new parts of his adopted country. Hell, before this assignment, he'd never entertained even a passing thought of visiting Richmond, Virginia. Even better, he was getting to do it in style. With an approving "Why not? What the hell?" from Will, he'd booked himself into the venerable Hotel Jefferson downtown, its wide, sweeping stairway the model for Tara's in *Gone With the Wind*, and shortly after his arrival in town, he'd treated himself to a guided tour of the Museum of the Confederacy, housed in the former Confederate White House, an 1818 townhouse regarded as just a cut below Mount Vernon and Monticello among historic Virginia dwellings.

Not that he was neglecting the task at hand—far from it, the work was always paramount—but Danny was rigorously methodical in his approach, always beginning at the beginning, with no preconceptions, and following every lead that showed even fleeting promise.

That's what had brought him to Grace Street this morning. According to the records he'd unearthed in the Virginia State Library, it was here that Francine Grabler, née Johnson, had grown up in the 1960s, the daughter of one Conrad Johnson, a foreman at the Epps and Sargent tobacco warehouse, and his wife Lucille, a housewife, originally from Roanoke. She had attended J. Floyd Preston elementary school and Patrick Henry High.

Preferring the old-fashioned ways, Danny had recorded these and a handful of other facts in the spiral-bound notebook he always carried in his breast pocket. But it was only the most rudimentary of beginnings. He'd been unable to locate any record of a marriage or divorce—though given the fact of her name change, one could be presumed and the other was likely. Nor, oddly, had a single article mentioning the native daughter's activities in the realms of publishing, academia or social activism turned up in the archives of either the *Richmond Times Dispatch* or the defunct *News Leader*.

It was of course possible, even likely, that because Grabler's accomplishments, such as they were, had occurred long after she'd left Richmond, they simply failed to draw the sort of prideful attention that they would have in the progressive hotbeds of the Northeast.

Yet he also could not discount the possibility that the surprising absence of information was not entirely accidental. He'd had cases before in which the subject of inquiry, intent on constructing a new life, had set about deliberately obscuring an older, more troubling or embarrassing one.

He had arrived at the address in his notebook, 1326 W. Grace. The house bore the familiar marks of the Colonial revival, from the colonnade front to the decorative pediment over the front door. But it was narrower than most on the block, and was one of those that had not yet been refurbished.

Danny was looking it over when the front door opened and a pair of pretty young women carried their bicycles down the wooden steps to the walkway.

"How you doing?" Danny said, flashing a smile from the other side of the wrought-iron gate.

This was a relatively high crime neighborhood and they stopped without opening the gate.

"Okay," said the blonde tentatively.

"Just admiring your house."

"It's not ours, we just rent. Five of us."

He'd of course surmised that; the campus of Virginia Commonwealth University was close by, and he'd already remarked on the number of young people—and great looking women—in the neighborhood. "Happen to know who the architect was? Looks to me like it might've been Carl Ruehrmund. He did a lot of the buildings around here."

The girls exchanged a quick look that said *He's not dangerous, just weird.* "Noooo," said the blonde. "Sorry, wish we could help."

Sweet kids, Danny thought. *Wouldn't mind either one of them. Or both, simultaneously.*

"Appreciate it, anyway."

"Well, we gotta get to class," said her friend, the brunette. Kicking open the gate, she wheeled her bike through, followed by the blonde. "But, listen," she added, nodding toward the right, "if you want to see the really nice places in this neighborhood, try Monument Avenue."

"Thanks, I'll do that." Then, as the girls turned away. "Did you know someone famous used to live in your place?"

Looking back, they spoke simultaneously: "Who?"

"Francine Grabler. She's a writer... wrote some really important stuff."

"Never heard of her," said the brunette.

"She wrote about kindness... and victims."

She shrugged. "Still never heard—"

"Hey, wait," her friend said, the light bulb going bright. "Hold on!"

She opened her book bag, started rummaging, and pulled out an oversized paperback: *Pain and Anguish* and pointed to the name at the bottom: Francine Grabler. "Her! We're supposed to read it for Hu-Po, my Human Potentials class!"

"Exactly."

"Wow! Incredible!"

Over her shoulder, Danny was aware of an older woman, broom in hand, on the porch of the house two doors down. She'd stopped what she was doing to observe the scene.

The blonde was looking at the cover illustration, an abstract in bright red of some indeterminate animal—part cow, part fox, part snake—howling in agony. "Yeah, it's all about how *everything* feels pain—even plants." She indicated her friend. "That's why me and her stopped walking on the grass!"

"Well, she grew up right in this house."

"I'll tell Ms. Schneider." She smiled as they started off. "She'll be really excited. Thanks again."

"Hey," Danny called after, "hope it helps your grade!"

He paused just a moment before heading toward the woman on the porch. At his approach, she hurriedly resumed her sweeping.

"Excuse me, Ma'am," he called, unconsciously emulating the local dialect.

She looked up with an icy stare.

"I'm hoping you can help me...." She continued staring, so he smiled even wider. "Have you lived here very long?"

"Who wants to know?" she demanded, with an accent as syrupy as anyone he'd yet encountered around here.

"I'm looking for information about a family that used to live there." He gestured with his head. "Where those girls are now. The Johnsons?"

She hesitated. "I knew 'em all right."

"Nice people?"

"Not really."

"Ahh." He nodded, buying time. "Well, I'd surely be obliged if you could help me out. I've been hired by some relatives of theirs out in San Diego. There's a child with a medical condition, and they're looking for a genetic match. It's real important."

She hesitated, then decided. "Okay, then... might as well come inside."

* * * * *

Professor Kane moved determinedly down the corridor in Sharpe Hall, the building that housed the Electrical Engineering department, and exited through the massive oaks doors onto Archer Avenue. His students, Sergei and Than, trailed after, half-running to keep up.

For a few moments he seemed to be heading in the direction of Professor Grabler's office in Newkirk-Gore

Hall, and they were relieved when he veered off onto the quad. They'd both experienced Kane's temper first hand and knew the worst thing for him, and for his department, would be for him to get in that awful woman's face. But no, apparently he was just taking some air, as he often did when thinking things through.

Suddenly, he broke into a run, heading for the far end of the quad. It took a moment before they understood: some kid was after one of his *Stand Up For Liberty* signs. Sergei and Than had personally posted a first batch all over campus just yesterday, and already those were either down or defaced, with *Liberty* inked out and replaced by *White Male Privilege*. The one the kid was going for now was part of a smaller new batch, by Kane's order placed in places less readily accessible. This one was tacked to a tree a good ten feet off the ground, but the vandal had a stepladder and was at work with a Magic Marker.

Kane prided himself on carrying the same weight as back in his days in the Corps, and with being nearly as lithe, and his students were amazed at how fast their teacher could move. He was almost there by the time the kid in the tree noticed and, startled, jumped down and took off. But the kid was a lard-ass to start with, and further slowed by a pair of socially responsible jute sandals.

Kane closed fast. "Stop right there, you little bastard, or I'll rip you a new one!"

The kid slowed, then stopped and turned his way.

He was breathing heavily, and he was about to cry. "Don't hurt me!"

"*Hurt* you?" The idea was so preposterous, Kane laughed. This idiot was every bit as gullible as the Okinawans his father had faced in the Big One who had killed themselves en masse rather than fall into the hands of the Americans the Jap propaganda had lied to them about; he actually believed Grabler's pap.

By now, Kane's students had caught up.

"*Please,* I suffer from hyper-anxiety." The kid fumbled in his jeans pocket, produced a folded prescription. "I have dangerously high levels of cortisol."

"Stop your bellyaching! What the hell's wrong with you?" He indicated Than. "See this guy? He grew up in a goddamn cardboard box! You see him whining?"

As Kane drew closer, the kid fell to the ground, drawing himself into a ball, awaiting the blows sure to come.

"Actually, it was a trailer, professor," corrected Than.

Standing over the kid, Kane seemed not even to hear, nor had he noticed the dozen other students converging on the scene. "Don't they teach you anything?" He jerked a thumb up at the sign, with the word *Liberty* already half-inked out. "You *defend* liberty, you don't spit on it! And this *patriarchy* you fools are always going on about? Goddamnit, the root is Latin, *patrocinor*—to *protect*!"

The kid was still cowering on the ground, expecting the worst.

"To protect, Moron, not hurt!" said Kane. Disgustedly kicking some dead leaves in his direction, he turned to his two students. "C'mon, men, this loser's not worth a second more of our time."

As they walked off, he noticed half a dozen cell phones capturing the scene. Within minutes it would be another weapon in Grabler's arsenal.

"Jesus H. Christ," he muttered in disgust. "I tell you, men, it really makes a guy sympathize with old Henry II. 'Will no one rid me of this troublesome bitch!'"

* * * * *

"Looks like you could use some more iced tea."

Danny smiled amiably, cursing himself for having drained his last glass of the vile stuff so quickly. His teeth were tingling from the sugar, and if it came to that, where would he ever find a decent dentist in this town?

"Yes, Ma'am, I surely could. Best ever."

"We like to think so. Other people like to skimp on the sugar."

"Well, that's the whole point, isn't it?"

"Some people just don't like how we do things down here, doesn't matter what."

By now, Danny was keenly aware not just of Mrs. Abbott's feelings about Northerners, but of the undercurrent of resentment marking her entire life. She hadn't yet had an unqualified good word to say about anyone. Even her late husband, Grant, though a hard worker, was also something of a waste, having failed to avail himself of numerous work opportunities that might have left her, his widow, a lot less troubled about money than she was. Danny couldn't help but note that in their wedding photo, Grant, on leave from Korea and in his dress greens, looked like the happiest guy in the world, while she already appeared disappointed that he was the best she could do. Meanwhile, her married daughter had been unable to give her a grandchild; and if her irresponsible son, also named Grant, down in Columbia, South Carolina, had ever sired any kids, she didn't even want to know about it.

For all that, the business of gaining her trust seemed to be going well.

"Who's the sick child?" she asked, as soon as he was through the door.

"Her name's Lucy. She's six years old."

"What's she got?"

"It's called *monocytic ehrlichiosis*," he replied soberly. "An autoimmune disease, usually fatal." In fact, just a year before it had killed his own beloved border collie mix, Lucia, though of course he had no idea what, if anything, it did to humans. "Everyone's praying for her."

"Poor child."

"They're putting their faith in me, hoping against hope I can find a genetic match."

Still, he'd already been here a good forty-five minutes, had choked down two glasses of iced tea, admired her collection of angel figurines in the living room cabinet and listened to a chunk of her life story, and he hadn't even begun to get anything of value.

As she poured him another glass, she asked. "You getting paid for this?"

"Well, the family has hired me, if that's what you mean."

"How 'bout the Johnsons? If you find them, will they get money?"

So that was it. *Shameless, and with a child's life at stake! !Que puta egoísta!* Not that he wasn't grateful—anything to get things moving in the right direction. "I guess that'll be between them and the relatives. Usually people are pretty understanding in a situation like this."

"How 'bout if someone helps you find them?"

"That can sometimes be arranged," nodded Danny. "It's called a finder's fee. If the information is useful enough." He paused meaningfully. "Are you saying you know—"

"They were bad people. Trash!" In contrast to her put-downs of others, which were casual, just part of the lousy way the world worked, this came with some vehemence.

"How do you mean?"

"Trash," she repeated. "Ask me, the Johnsons'd never put themselves out for some kid, leastways not if there isn't something in it for them!"

"The father...." Danny checked his pad. "Conrad. According to what I have here, he worked in a warehouse down by the river."

"A drunk," she said adamantly. "A *mean* drunk."

"Violent?"

"What do you think? Used to beat the hell outta her and the kids too." She paused. "What does this have to do with getting their genes?"

"I need to know what we'll be dealing with, assuming I'm even able to locate them. It was a long time ago."

"It was, and they're probably dead and buried. Not that I guess anyone's mourning."

"How long ago you figure they moved away?"

She gazed upward, calculating. "Gotta be thirty years at least. Wait, forty's probably more like it. Lord, God, am I that old?"

Danny made a show of jotting it down in his pad.

"But Conrad, he left a long time before then."

"Divorced?"

"Divorced?" She snorted in incredulity. "Just up and left. People said there was another woman. After that, she did all her drinking alone."

"So she was also a drunk...."

"That's what I'm telling you."

"Okay. Got it." He paused, went for it. "What about the children, the son and daughter?"

"Robert, he took after the father." She took a sip of tea, then elaborated. "Mean. Bullied around all the younger children. My husband and me made sure Grant kept outta his way. Which wasn't easy, them living so close."

"Like what sorts of things would he do?"

"Just a bully. Liked to make other kids cry."

"Pretty awful."

"And, you know, stick firecrackers on tails of stray cats, things like that. Nothing to call the police over, but just *mean.*"

"I see." Danny nodded. *Nothing serious, only the classic makings of a future serial killer.*

"That's around the time they left, after Robert got killed."

"He was killed? How?"

"In Vietnam. Don't look so surprised, it's not like he was the only one. They say they gave him some kind'a big medal for bravery."

"I see." He glanced down at the pad again. "And what about the little sister... Francine?"

"What about her?"

"Well, it's a good bet she'd be the only one left."

"She was just like the rest."

Danny couldn't hide his surprise. "Really?"

"In a different way, maybe, but just as bad. She's the one we knew best 'cause my daughter's around the same age. Just a real nasty girl."

"So your daughter knew her pretty well."

She nodded. "When they were little... five, six, seven, around like that. After that, she wanted nothing to do with the Johnson girl."

"Why's that?"

"She was another bully—used to bring a little metal thimble to school, and in assembly she'd flick the kids sitting in front of her in the head. Julia'd tell me about it. Said it hurt like the bejeezus, and Francine would just laugh."

He shook his head sympathetically.

"Another time, she stuck the branch of a rose bush right down the back of Julia's dress, with all the prickers on it. That was when I sent my husband over there to see the Johnsons, not that it did any good. That little girl of theirs just stood there, bold as brass, and lied to his face."

"What'd your husband do?"

"Nothin', it was her word against Julia's. Besides, he was also miffed at Julia 'cause he thought she should've stuck up for herself."

"I see."

"She just had it in for Julia 'cause Julia was real popular, and naturally the way she was, Francine wasn't. And then, later on in high school, Francine was a real tramp, so of course she hated Julia even more." She hesitated. "She did some things... I can't even talk about them."

"I understand." He waited a moment to see if this was so. When she volunteered nothing further, he leaned intently forward. "You wouldn't happen to know what happened to her? If she ever got married, for instance."

She gave a short, bitter laugh. "I don't doubt some men promised her that to get what they wanted. Otherwise...." She shook her head. "Around here it's different from where you come from. Girls know what young men want in a wife. At least, they used to."

"I only ask because she seems to have changed her name at some point."

"Well, I wouldn't know about that."

"So you have no idea what became of her?"

"No... but I'm thinking we could ask Julia."

"Absolutely, if it's not too much bother."

"She and her husband are down by Danville. I could call her for you."

"That's fine, but I'm perfectly happy to call her myself."

"I'd best be calling her first," she said meaningfully, "so she'll know to expect it. And also about the finding fee."

"That's fine," Danny said, caught short, having momentarily forgotten that particular lie. "That would be very helpful."

She wrote down her daughter's number for him in pencil on the back of an envelope. "When you talk to her, best not bring up high school. What the Johnson girl did, it was just *rude*."

"It's a sore subject, I understand."

To soothe his conscience, before leaving he handed her a fifty, the sum total of Marty Katz's dough that would be coming her way. But then, just to be sure she followed through, he said, "Think of it as a down payment."

* * * * *

Will had looked forward to the meeting with all the pleasure of a visit to the dentist. His philosophy was as straightforward as they come—never give the bastards an inch—yet here he was, on his own initiative, giving away the whole store.

Until the last minute, he was thinking of calling it off. Strategy be damned, he truly didn't know whether he could sit across the table from these two jackasses for more than five seconds without losing it—not just his temper but a large glass of V-8, a blueberry muffin, an *All-the-Way* lox sandwich (cream cheese, tomato, double chives), two cups of coffee, plus the usual take-out order of extra-crisp bacon he'd finished here at the office; the entire exceptionally satisfying breakfast he'd enjoyed this morning *gratis* at the Euclid Diner.

His hands were still greasy when the phony Indian and his lawyer showed up, but that didn't stop Will from shaking their hands.

"Thanks for coming, gents," he said, smiling. "Bygones and all that, right?"

It was hard to tell who was more suspicious, Larry Harris or his weasel-for-hire Joel Gitlin, staring down in disgust at his greasy hand.

"We're just here to listen," Gitlin said sourly.

"So, Mr. Harris...." Will turned to address the Indian. "Mr. 3-X Perkins here tells me you two had a good talk." He nodded at Arthur, already seated at the firm's new conference table, an AOD find until recently located in the dining niche of a one-bedroom in Washington Heights.

"You don't have to answer that," Gitlin said.

"It wasn't a question, Joel, just an observation," Will said mildly, holding his smile.

In fact, it had taken Arthur most of a week to track Harris down. Not only did he never show up at work, he never seemed to sleep at the decrepit Greenpoint studio apartment listed as his home address; and it was only through efforts worthy of the most skillful of Harris's purported ancestors that Arthur managed to find him in a Blarney Stone bar in Astoria, Queens. There, as instructed, he'd immediately begun laying on the firewater, and soon Harris was spouting off to the sympathetic young black man not only about the abuse he suffered at the hands of a certain *bastard Jew cocksucker landlord* but about his own *useless Jew lawyer*.

While it was safe to presume the Indian wouldn't remember any of it, Will had the tape in his pocket, and was just itching to give Harris's attorney a listen. A classic Legal Aid type, Gitlin had been his adversary through all of Katz's travails with this deadbeat scumbag of an employee, and he'd come to loathe him even more than he loathed his client. Once, after an especially grueling day facing off against him in court, he'd ostentatiously opened his Miriam-Webster dictionary to the word *twerp—a silly, insignificant or contemptible person*—to show he'd pasted a photo of Gitlin alongside.

Now he flashed his most ingratiating smile. "I understand, Mr. Harris, you had quite a bit to say the other day. Anyway, that's what Mr. 3-X Perkins tells me, isn't it, Arthur?"

Trying to make himself invisible, the black associate nodded. "Yes, Sir."

"Mr. 3X Perkins approached my client under false pretenses!" Gitlin snapped. "So if you don't have a damn good reason for getting us here, we'll see you in court!"

"Calm down, Joel. Why so antagonistic?" Will indicated a couple of seats at the table. "I asked you here in good faith. I think we can help each other."

"We'll see about that," he replied, but both he and Harris took seats. "This better be good."

"Arthur tells me you weren't easy to locate, Larry," Will said to the Indian. "May I call you Larry? Or would you prefer...." He almost gagged. "Your Native American name?"

"You don't have to answer that," said Gitlin. Then, to Will, "*Mister* Harris, same as in court. Tripp, don't even bother pretending you appreciate the richness of Native American culture."

"My only point is that we've gone to great lengths to arrange this *pow wow*, if you will." He answered Gitlin's hateful look with a smile. "It is our earnest and sincere desire to finally put all this unpleasantness behind us. Trust me, you won't be sorry you came." He nodded reassuringly. "And, hey, if nothing comes of it, no loss. You can just go after poor Arthur here for harassment or intimidation or whatever else your ferret brain conjures up."

"All right, we're here," he said irritably. "Let's hear your proposal."

Will hesitated. *God, how I loathe these two.* "Joel," he said, leaning back in his chair, "remember when things got really ugly between us?"

He looked puzzled. "I *never* liked you, Tripp. You represent everything I despise."

"Noted. Without prejudice. Right back at you. However sick you're made by the very sight of me, I got it twice as bad." He smiled. "It was the very first time my client, Marty Katz, tried to get your friend here fired for relieving himself while on duty."

"I peed on a little kid in the lobby," recalled the Indian evenly. "I had to go bad."

"Just so. Because, as attorney Gitlin so ably argued before the city's Civil Rights Commission, reaching the toilet available for the purpose constituted an undue hardship. You'd have had to go through a door and walk down a long hallway, which might have taken as long as twenty-five seconds."

"Exactly!" said Gitlin, recalling the case.

"What's more, it was established to the Commission's satisfaction that *you,* Mr. Harris, were in fact the victim in the matter, since the child's ostentatious display of wealth and overweening sense of privilege left you at that moment feeling deeply shamed and humiliated."

"Economic injustice," Gitlin said softly, nodding. "If you look closely enough, it's there in almost every case."

"Yes! I raise this now because at this moment we find ourselves with a common enemy. Namely, those filthy rich tenants in the building—most of whom, by the way, quite frankly, are equal-opportunity haters. We've learned through sad experience that they are as intolerant of landlords and dwarves every bit as much as of Native Americans and drunks. Excuse me, let me rephrase—as persons afflicted with dipsomania."

The others looked at him with interest, awaiting more.

"And why? Because we're all seen as different, The Other."

"Well," Gitlin started, at something of a loss. "It's good to hear you finally admit it... at least as far as Mr. Harris is concerned and—"

"Fuckin' bastards!" blurted out Harris.

Will placed a hand on Arthur's shoulder. "And if it makes any difference, Mr. 3-X Perkins assures me they don't much care for people of color either."

His associate shot him a bewildered, what-does-this-have-to-do-with-me look.

"Okay, Tripp, you got our attention. What's the bottom line?"

Will slid from his chair and walked to his desk drawer. Pulling out a sheet of paper, he returned to the table. "I think this would be a good place to start," he said, sliding it toward Gitlin.

The lawyer studied it a long moment. "'No formal responsibilities.' What exactly does that mean?"

"He'll have full salary and benefits, regular raises built in, and he'll no longer have to come to work. Plus all the booze he can get his mitts on from Apartments of the Dead, or the apartments of the living, for all we care. Basically, you win."

"No responsibilities?"

"Only that he might be called upon from time to time to make an appearance before an official body or representative of the legal system." He turned to the Indian. "You're used to doing that already, right?"

He nodded. "I like going to court. They treat me good."

"And that, in this context, he might very occasionally, under exceptional circumstances, be asked to contribute his unique perspective," added Will.

Gitlin stared hard at the paper.

"There's no catch, Joel."

"This paperwork is just preliminary. I'll want to see a final draft."

"Of course." Will nodded. "Accept it. We've thrown in the towel. You've won."

"Well, then!" He allowed himself a tentative smile and turned to his client. "What do you think? Maybe time to break out the peace pipe?"

* * * * *

"Why don't you two just relax," said Julia Clarke, nee Abbott, "and I'll fetch some of my famous iced tea."

"You do that, Hon," said her husband Clint.

"Mmm, sounds delicious," added Danny, hoping against hope she'd drastically altered her mother's recipe.

"Good woman," Clint said admiringly, watching his wife disappear through the door. "I've been blessed."

"I can see that." From his perch on the sofa, Danny glanced around the room, simply decorated but immaculate. The place was a single-story ranch, two bedrooms, two baths, that he figured to be from the mid-'70s. "So how long have you lived in Danville?"

"Since '90. Got the house right before Jeannette came into our lives."

"Ah."

A mountainous 300-pounder in a work shirt with a logo for Columbia Gas and loose pants that failed to obscure his gut, Clint suddenly got to his feet, returning a moment later cradling a framed photograph from the mantle. "This is her," he said gently.

Danny looked down at the pretty young black woman in the graduation gown. Mrs. Abbott had gone on at some length about Julia and Clint, but it took no flash of insight to know why she'd never so much as mentioned her adopted granddaughter.

"She's beautiful," he said, meaning it.

Clint nodded. "The light of our lives."

"What's she up to now?"

"She's doin' real good—she's up in Chesterfield County... works in Special Ed."

"She's fixing to be married one of these days," Julia added, coming through the door with a tray. "Not that they seem about to set a date."

"Don't worry, Hon, they will."

"Chesterfield County... that's up near Richmond, isn't it?"

"That's right, not too far," Julia said, setting down the tray.

"Near her grandmother," Danny observed mildly, and watched them exchange a look. Danny had a conscience, but sentiment was a luxury; he'd been here a quarter hour already, and had to get things moving in the right direction. "She was very helpful to me, your mother."

"They don't actually see too much of each other," Julia said, not taking the hint as she poured him a cup of lemonade.

"Or any," Cliff said. "Her loss, is how we look at it. Jeannette feels the same way."

Danny took a sip. It was, if anything, viler than her mother's.

"My mom is just so darned...." Julia searched for right word. "*Silly* sometimes... but you know, she grew up in different times, and she's had a real hard life besides. A lot of folks back then felt the same way... some a lot worse."

"Of course." Hell, if some family member of his ever refused to acknowledge any kid of his, that would be it, end of story.

"Family can be real hard, Danny," she said, as if reading his mind. "But as Christians, we work every day to live out our creed. And when it's hard... well, what's the use of having a creed that's easy?"

"I guess that's true," he said.

"Just 'cause someone's wrong don't make them evil. Don't mean you stop loving them."

There was a long silence.

Clint said, "Jeannette, she wants to have a big blowout, and we sure can't afford it." He smiled. "Not unless we hit the lottery."

"I hear you," Danny said blandly. *Okay, fine, here we go*. "I guess your mother told you why I wanted to see you."

"She said something about paying us to talk about some old school friend of Julia's."

"Francine Johnson, a neighbor girl," Julia said.

"Sounded a little fishy to me."

"Didn't she also tell you why we're looking for her?"

"*Why?* No...."

Danny could hardly believe it. *What a monster. She talked about the money, but not the phony critically ill child!* With urgency, he said, "It's because we need a genetic match!" He went on to explain about the little girl in San Diego and her desperate parents.

Julia and Clint listened with deep sympathy.

"Sounds pretty bad," Clint said, when he was done.

"I'm afraid it is."

"What's the disease again?"

"Monocytic ehrlichiosis," he replied a bit guiltily.

"Never heard of it."

"It's pretty rare." Then, somberly, "Also afflicts animals, I understand."

"I think I heard about it on Oprah," said Julia. "Or maybe Dr. Phil. One of 'em."

"Probably."

"Wait, hold on!" She went to the bookshelf and picked up a volume lying flat upon the others in the middle shelf. "I got it out yesterday, after Mommy called," she said, holding it aloft. "Our yearbook."

It was brown imitation leather and embossed with *The Patriot, 1975*.

Danny reached for it, but she playfully slapped his hand. "I'll *show* you."

She flipped to the photos of the graduating seniors and pointed. "See if you know who this is."

It couldn't have been more obvious. "You?"

"Right! But just look at that hair!"

Clint said, "You're still beautiful, Julia."

"Thank you, Hon," she said with a smile, then turned to Danny. "See how well trained he is? He has to say that or else."

"No, it's true, you really do look young."

"Well, thank you, kind sir." She flipped a few pages ahead, then stopped and pointed. "Here she is... Francine."

This one really was a surprise. He'd never have guessed this was the same person as the dragon lady in the shot Will had shown him. It wasn't just her altogether pleasant expression, or even the hair, in a wave more suggestive of a would-be prom princess than Medusa. In fact, with her wide set eyes and full lips this girl was pretty, even *sexy*.

"Is that really what she looked like?"

"Well, sort of. She must've spent hours getting her hair to look like that. And she never used to smile."

Danny noted that beneath the photo there was no list of clubs or organizations, as there was for everyone else, and that the quotation she'd chosen—*Useless, useless*—came with no attribution. He pointed at it. "You know what that's supposed to mean?"

She shrugged. "No idea."

"Your mother said you had some problems with her, in high school especially."

"Not just me, a lot of people did."

"She said she did something to you that was especially hurtful."

She thought for just an instant, then smiled. "Oh, that. It was no big deal really. Clint knows about it, don't you, Hon?"

"I'm not sure what you're talking about."

"Oh, you know, she was the girl that started the rumor that Betsy Crandall and I were... you know."

"More than friends?" offered Danny gently.

"Of course, it was a big lie. Betsy and me were cheerleaders and pretty popular, and I guess Francine was jealous. No one believed it, but for a while there it was pretty hard on my mom."

"So you never confronted her about it?"

"No. What was the point?" She paused. "Thinking about it now, she was just such a sad thing, so lost. She was probably angry like she was 'cause that's what she learned at home."

Danny nodded, recognizing an Oprah fan when he saw one. "What about boys?"

She laughed. "Oh, she had plenty of those, all right."

"She's saying she was easy," Clint said.

"Boys took advantage of her?"

"Or maybe more like the other way around. Francine could be pretty aggressive in that area, if you know what I mean." She caught herself. "Sorry, that was unkind. I wasn't there, so I don't really know."

"Anyway, it sounds like you haven't had too much contact with her lately."

"None really. Not since high school."

"Can you think of anyone who might've?"

"Well, lemme see...." She began flipping through the faces. "Wait, yes!" She flipped ahead and pointed to a photo of a singularly unattractive girl named Claudia Mackey.

"Claudia!" said Julia decisively. "She and Francine were tight as Francine got with anyone. Both were, you know...."

"Losers," offered her husband.

"Royal screw-ups, anyway. Used to cut class together."

In the shot, Claudia was wearing a white blouse with a Peter Pan collar, but there was no attempt at a smile, and the eyes in her thin, pock-marked face were lifeless. If he'd spotted her in the street, he'd have pegged her for a runaway strung out on heroin.

"Have any idea where she might be now?" From the looks of it, *dead* was a serious possibility.

"I know *exactly*—me and her reconnected a few years ago on Classmates.com."

"She can't get enough of those social media doodads," teased Clint.

"That's not so, Clint, I just like to keep up with the times." She turned back to Danny. "From what I can tell, she's doing good. Really straightened herself out. She's down in Florida, somewhere around Sarasota."

"Think she'll talk to me?"

"I don't see why not; she's real nice."

Though twenty minutes later, as Danny was leaving, they exacted a promise to let them know what happened with the sick little girl, they never once mentioned money.

And that evening, there was one more surprise. Looking it up on the web, he discovered that "Useless, useless" were the dying words of John Wilkes Booth.

* * * * *

"Oh God, oh God, oh God!!"

The cameraman moved in tighter on the stricken young woman as she buried her face in her Chester College sweatshirt and began sobbing openly.

"I'm sorry," she managed.

"That's okay," gently soothed the pretty blonde reporter, just off camera. "We all understand."

"How could it happen?" asked the girl in anguish. *"How?"*

Always intrigued by the media's ability to harness emotion for maximum effect—a skill he was looking to improve upon himself—Will watched closely. On his fingers he counted the beats—one, two, three—as the camera held the devastated girl, before it slowly moved left and upward to capture the cause of her distress.

Already nearly a dozen investigators were at the crime scene, a neat, two story clapboard house fronted by a pair of oak trees. Beyond the yellow tape strung out across the sidewalk could be seen not only heavily armed state troopers and CSI types, but the cream of the Chester PD, all of them grimly watched over by the four-person campus security force in their distinctive tie-dyed shorts, Nerf clubs in hand.

"Yes, *how?*" picked up the reporter, as she slowly walked toward the house, Will listening in at a discreet distance. "That's the question everyone is asking on this bucolic, once-tranquil campus in the rolling hills of majestic upstate New York. *How*, but also *why?* And *who?* What kind of deranged individual—or individuals—could have done such a thing?" She paused, then said ominously, "I must warn you, some of what we are about to show is very disturbing, and not fit for younger children."

She paused a moment, as the cameraman began slowly panning the graffiti-marred house. "This is the home, at the edge of the Chester campus, of Dr. Francine Grabler, Chester's Distinguished Professor of Oppression Studies. This happened sometime last night, or early this morning."

The reporter fell silent, letting the horrific images tell the story. The camera focused first on *BITCH*, scrawled diagonally in angry, uneven black capital letters down the side of the house, clearly the product of a disordered mind; then it moved to *BITCH-Liar*, the second word in smaller letters; then to *SCREW VICTIMS*. The *coup de grace* was off to the side: *COCKS RULE*. The monster had added a small illustration of a penis firing bullets. Finally, in the far corner appeared what seemed to have been a hurried and unfinished afterthought: *SUCK MY D....*

"Make no mistake," the reporter said soberly, "this is a terrorist attack, and that's how it has been classified by the authorities. Whoever did this came here last night armed with a weapon more toxic than any poison gas. The weapon of hate.

"Nor, I must sadly report, was the victim—a title Professor Grabler wears as a badge of honor—chosen at random. She is a beloved figure not only here at Chester

College, where she has made the fight against hatred and intolerance her personal crusade, but among fighters for tolerance and understanding nation-wide. For now, understandably, she is in seclusion and under a doctor's care.

"Who committed this unspeakable act?" the reporter continued. "Was it outsiders? Or might it, quite possibly, be someone within this very community? Unfortunately, as investigators and school officials look for answers on this terrible day, they refuse to discount this last possibility."

So there it is, Will thought. *Rather than protecting their own or simply clamming up, the Chester administration is pointing fingers.* The only question was whether Bennett was among those they were prepared to throw overboard.

"Grief counselors are on the scene," the reporter continued, "giving solace to the many students and staff shaken by this tragedy, and administration sources assure me that more will be made available as needed." She paused meaningfully. "What is both ironic, yet at this moment seems oddly appropriate, is that Chester's president, Warren Frank, with whom I spoke just a few moments ago, has long made *healing* his watchword. Healing the planet. Healing the rifts between nations and peoples. Healing the broken parts of individual souls.

"For all his good works, President Frank tells me he now faces his most daunting challenge of all—healing his own shattered community. Becky Baker, WFUN-NEWS, Albany."

She waited a moment; then, off the air, spoke again, "How was that?" A beat, as she listened to a voice in her earpiece. "Good, thanks." She listened again, then more sharply said, "Okay, but listen up—when you cut in the Frank interview for the 5:00 piece, be sure to use that moment when he tears up." A beat. "Yeah, I know it's obvious, but you can never be too sure. And make it clear the interview's an exclusive."

"Tell them to cut in that shot of the kid on the cell phone," the cameraman suggested.

"Hear that? Alex says to maybe run footage of the kid who lost it talking to her mom on the cell. Anyway, listen, we'll keep getting you updates from here 'cause we gotta stay up front on this one!"

"Nice work," the cameraman said, when she was off with the studio. "It'll be terrific on your reel."

"Better be," she said, setting aside the microphone. "How many of *these* turn up in our own backyard? But look." She nodded sourly in the direction of the news vans lined up across the way in the parking lot, several of them lately arrived all the way from the big city. "These guys are jackals, and we've got a feeding frenzy."

"Right." The cameraman laughed. "And we're just little baby jackals. Want a beer?"

"Jesus, Alex, it's not even 9:00 a.m."

"And that's a problem, why?" he said, and started off.

She'd just pulled a compact from her bag when she was aware of the small man looking up at her.

"Great report!"

"Thank you," she said, recovering from her surprise. "That's one story I wish I didn't have to tell."

"I know," he empathized. "Tough job you've got."

"It can be." She snapped her compact shut and pulled her bag over her shoulder. "Well, back to work."

"Think they know who did it?"

"Sorry, no time," she said curtly, and started off.

"Hey," he called after her, loudly, "I guess two minutes is too much to ask from a big celebrity like you."

She wheeled, looking down at him with loathing; *How dare this little shit talk to me that way*! But, as always, she was aware of the possibility of others taking note, and shot him her on-camera smile. "Forgive me," she said, extending her hand. "I'm Becky."

"Will," he said magnanimously, taking it. "No hard feelings. I guess you're just on edge today like the rest of us."

"Yes."

"Personally, I got almost no sleep last night."

"Uh huh."

Seeing she was just waiting for the chance to disengage, he added, "I got up here as soon as I heard—had to charter a plane."

"Excuse me?" she said with sudden interest. You *chartered* a plane? Why?"

"I live downstate. But my brother, he teaches here. I wanted to be sure to be here for him when he woke up and got the news."

She nodded, sniffing an angle and drew him aside. "So you chartered a *private* plane? You must love your brother very much."

"I do. He's been going through a real tough time and, well, you know, I've looked out for him my whole life and I knew how hard this would hit him and—"

"Wait," she said, putting up a hand. "If you don't mind, I'd love to get this on camera. Would that be all right?"

"Sure, why not?"

Hurriedly glancing around, she spotted the cameraman. He had a beer in one hand, and with the other was shooting a bunch of female students, backs heaving as they engaged in an intense group hug. "Hey, Alex!" she called.

He didn't hear, or pretended not to, and it occurred to her that the kids' grief interested him less than getting those tight co-ed asses for his private collection.

"Alex!"

This time he turned her way. She was vigorously motioning him toward her.

As he approached, she led Will around a corner and further out of view. She had him stand in front of a wall and positioned herself on a slight rise alongside, emphasizing even more his modest stature. At the cameraman's signal, she knelt to lower the mic to Will's level. "Now, then, Will here tells me he actually *chartered an airplane* to be with his brother on this terrible morning."

"Yes, I did, Becky."

"And you say your brother teaches here at Chester College?"

"Yes, he has for many years, and I knew how upset he'd be by what's happened."

"And what does he teach here at Chester?"

"Physics."

"I see...." She paused, something going on behind her baby blues. "And what's your brother's name?"

"Bennett. Bennett Tripp. We've always been extremely close."

Even someone who hadn't been listening for it might well have caught her sudden change in tone. " Well, thank you very much, Will. Good luck to you and your brother both."

"That's it?" he asked, when the camera was off.

"I think we got what we need." She paused, then caught him by surprise. "Do you suppose you might be able to arrange for me to ask Bennett a few questions?"

* * * * *

"Lillian's Fine Antiques, this is Miss Mackey, how may I be of service?"

Sitting in his shorts on an unmade bed in his room in The Fiddler's Inn outside Keeling, Virginia, Danny's first thought was that maybe there was some kind of mistake. It seemed almost inconceivable that the syrupy sweet voice on the other end of the line belonged to the sullen and hard-bitten street kid from the high school yearbook.

"*Claudia* Mackey?"

"This is she. May I inquire as to whom I am speaking?"

"My name is Danny Valenzuela. Julia Clarke suggested I call."

"Julia Clarke!" she exclaimed. "How *is* that sweet thing?"

"She's well. I saw her just this afternoon. So I gather you haven't yet heard from her?"

"I always liked her so much, Julia," she said, ignoring the question. "Not a stuck up bone in her body."

"I know, she's very nice."

"So classy. And such a pretty little thing."

It was like he was talking to one of those strange Southern women he'd hitherto experienced only via Tennessee Williams on Turner Classic Movies.

"Well, she sends her regards." He paused. "Listen, I know you're at work so—"

"Oh, never mind that. Sometimes whole days go by without a soul coming into this place. I'm just sitting here reading my Marianne Williamson."

"I see. So this would be a good time to talk?"

"*The Law of Divine Compensation*. So inspirational. Oh, yes, I have all the time in the world."

So, more or less, did he. And based on what he'd already heard, he knew how to proceed—at a leisurely pace, letting her take the lead. He'd met her type before, and Claudia was a grade-A specimen: alone and desperately eager for anything resembling human contact. The ones that made such ready prey for unscrupulous phone hucksters. Living, breathing Eleanor Rigbys.

"So tell me a little about yourself, Claudia."

That was all it took. Placing an extra pillow against the headboard, he settled back and began distractedly playing Words With Friends on his iPad, as she launched into her sad, checkered history.

He was right, she had been strung out, though not in high school (when living with her abusive mother), but soon after; she'd been addicted to meth and living on the streets in Norfolk. She endured several failed rehabs before one finally took, followed by a ten-year marriage to an abusive husband who wouldn't work before she finally straightened out thanks to a clinic in New Orleans and afterward found the courage to kick the husband to the curb. And she confided all of it in her oddly sweet and upbeat sing-song to a total stranger.

For his part, Danny had only to respond with an occasional "Just terrible" or "Good for you" to hold up his end.

She'd just gotten to her move to Florida back in '05, when a text arrived from Will: *Problem on this end. Need dirt on our girl ASAP*.

She'd been talking for a couple of minutes solid, and he waited a moment before interrupting. "Pardon me, Claudia?"

"Oh, I'm just talking your ear off, aren't I?" she said immediately, full of self-reproach. "I do that, I know."

"Oh, no, it's all really interesting," her new friend said. "Really. In fact, I lived in New Orleans for a while myself."

"Did you now!" she exclaimed, and he was sure she was about to take off again.

"But there's really something else I need to ask you about," he said quickly. "Something important."

"Important?" she said. "Whatever could *that* be?"

"It's about your old friend Francine."

There was a pause. "Francine Johnson?"

"I'm eager to find her and I've been looking for leads. Julia thought of you."

Once again, he went into the story of the desperately ill child, so familiar now he was almost starting to believe it himself.

"Oh, isn't that just the saddest thing?"

"This possible genetic match, that's really the last hope."

"Francine Johnson... goodness, I don't really know how much I can help."

"It's just that Julia said you were pretty close back in high school."

She hesitated, then softly chuckled. "We were quite the little pair of hell raisers. Did she tell you that?"

"Not in so many words."

"Well, that's Julia for you. She was never mean and vicious like a lot of the others."

"I know what high school can be like," he said, commiserating.

"It was pretty bad. I was lost. I had a lot of hate in my heart. But at least I had Francine. We had each other, me and her."

"For security?"

"And protection. Francine could be pretty tough in the girl's room. She gave as good as she got." She laughed. "Not that we were in school all that much. Lord, God, how we hated that place!"

He couldn't help but be struck by the change in her tone. As she relived those times it was sharper, the sing-songy quality all but gone.

"So you cut a lot?"

"All the time. We'd go over to the University of Richmond and smoke weed with the boys over there." She laughed again. "And oh my, our grades! I think they let us graduate just to be sure we wouldn't come back."

Danny chuckled in sympathy. "I saw what she put under her picture in the yearbook."

"Oh, yes, that! Did you see what's under mine?"

"Actually, no, I didn't notice."

"It was all Francine's idea, she wanted us to be a sort'a matched set. *Sic semper tyrannus*—that's what Mr. Booth shouted after he shot the president, it means tyrants should die. Lord, how we hated that place!" She paused. "We did some pretty wild things, the two of us."

"I can tell."

"Just terrible, the pair of us. It's embarrassing even to talk about it."

He laughed. "Hey, I've been there. So... any idea at all what became of her?"

"I just hope she's found peace, is all. She wasn't really a bad girl, just real confused. She was a seeker, like I am."

"Uh huh."

"Last time I saw her was maybe a couple of years after high school. She came down to Norfolk to see me. She'd stayed up in Richmond, but she was planning to go off to college."

"Really? Do you know where?"

"Not a real college... a whatchamacallit... a junior college, that's it. She showed me the catalogue. It was far away... way out West. She wanted me to go there with her. She said it was cheap and they had lots of drugs and they'd take about anyone 'cause it was just starting up."

"It was in California?"

"No, Arizona or New Mexico, one of those places. Phoenix maybe. I was a little fuzzy around then. I remember they had a picture of an old airplane hangar on the cover, which struck me as funny. That's where they were going to hold the classes."

"So you never saw her after that?"

"I think I wrote her a couple of letters, but I never got anything back."

"Well," he said a few minutes later, posturing to extricate himself. "I can't tell you how much I appreciate it."

"I hope it helps."

"It really does. Thank you."

"If you find Francine, will you please tell her hi for me?"

"Of course."

"I just hope she found what I never did: a good man."

In his room, Danny smiled, picturing Grabler. "Right."

"Tell her if she wants, she can give me a call."

* * * * *

"I was here with Casey," Bennett said. "Wednesday nights she stays over, remember?"

Will hadn't, though it was he who'd set the arrangement. "Did you go out, or just hang around here?"

"Where would we go?"

"How 'bout Chuck E. Cheese or someplace... isn't that where other guys take their kids?"

"What kind of father do you think I am?" demanded Bennett, indignant. "You really think I'd feed a child of mine that junk?" He shook his head vehemently. "Chuck E. Cheese!"

Will never ceased to be astonished by his brother. *After all that's happened, this is what rouses him to anger.* "You've probably never even been there," he said evenly. "Despite what the snobocracy says, it's really good."

"As if you'd know. Like Mom always said, put enough ketchup on it and you'd eat dog food."

"Fine," Will said, exasperated. "What you're telling me is you didn't go out at all."

He shook his head. "I made her risotto Milanese here."

Talk about child abuse, Will thought. *They should fire your ass just for that.* "Okay, got it. So we're gonna have to rely for corroboration on a four-and-a-half year old."

"Oh, c'mon, Will, you don't honestly think they'd try to—"

"No?" he exploded, no longer restraining himself. "What is *wrong* with you, Bennett? What goes on in that head of yours?"

"But I was here with Casey!" wailed Bennett. "There's no way they could ever accuse me of—"

"Wake up, you stupid fuck! There's more common sense on the average stall wall in a Chuck E. Cheese men's room than in all the lecture halls of that college of yours put together! I'm trying to save your ass here!"

"I'm just saying there's no evidence," protested Bennett.

"Like that matters! They don't *need* evidence! Just so you know, your distinguished president's already dropping hints to reporters, throwing out names of likely candidates."

"Me?"

"All I know is that I was talking to Becky Baker—"

"Becky Baker? From Channel 12?"

"And she seemed to have a pretty good idea of who you were. She wants to talk to you."

"She does?" he said, brightening. "Becky Baker?"

Will shook his head. "That's *not* gonna happen, Bro."

"Why not?" He looked at him imploringly. "You said you wanted me to meet new women."

"Do you *not* understand she's a journalist, which is a less-polite way of saying a fucking predator. She's looking to nail you, and not in the preferred sense of the term."

Looking deeply downcast, Bennett nodded.

Will sighed, put a hand on his brother's shoulder. "I have just one question for you, Bennett, and I need you to think about it carefully before you answer."

Bennett looked down at him.

"If it comes to that, are you ready to fight this thing all out? Go to the mattresses?"

"Will, you know I'm not like that."

"I know what you're like; that's why I'm asking you," he said, as his phone began to vibrate in his jacket pocket. "This is about to get seriously ugly, and I need to know you won't wimp out on me."

Bennett looked indescribably sad. "Will, this has been my world for a long time. These people are my colleagues and—"

"That's exactly what I'm talking about! When are you gonna finally grow a pair?"

He snatched the phone from his pocket. "Yeah?" He paused. "Christ! Well, all right, you're on."

He snapped the phone shut and turned back to his brother. "They've suspended classes for tomorrow; they're putting on another rally. For healing. What is it with these idiots and their rallies?"

"Maybe that's not such a bad thing; maybe it'll do some good."

"Yeah, that's probably it," Will said with depthless scorn. "And afterward a bunch of angels'll deliver Angelina Jolie in her birthday suit to your bed."

"All right," he said miserably. "I get it. Who was that who called?"

"Barbara Ann Doyle. She's gonna be my date at the rally."

"Her?" he said, in horror. "That... that *bitch?"*

Will nodded, pleased to see his brother showing at least a smidgen of fight. "Thataway," he said. "Only remember, you're gonna need all the friends you can get."

* * * * *

Over the years, the hunt had led Danny to a great many new places, but never had a strange place seemed so oddly familiar. Looking out over the surrounding desert terrain, with its stately saguaros and squat golden barrels, the low mountains looming beyond and the sun hotter than hell, he might have been in Chiapas, the village where he spent the first miserable fourteen years of his life. Except there were no shanties or gutters full of rotting refuse, but modern buildings, most utilizing the latest green technologies.

Claudia had been mistaken, but not by much: Oracle Junior College was not in Phoenix, but on the outskirts of Tucson. By his reckoning, Johnson/Grabler would've arrived here in either 1976, the year the place opened or, more likely, 1977. The same catalogue served for both years, its cover graced by the photo of the old airplane hangar Claudia so vividly recalled; it was a nod to the site's prior history as an air base.

The data on the school's early years were available on primitive printouts in the school library. A total of 3,543 students were registered for the fall '77 term, the overwhelming majority were Arizonans and most of them locals. But there were also almost four hundred of out-of-staters, and one of those was indeed Francine Johnson. The postage-sized headshot of her in the directory was the same one as in her high school yearbook.

Yet as he pored over the records of the period—lists of students' majors in assorted disciplines, members of athletic teams and college musical groups, winners of academic awards—he could find nothing else. There was no mention of Francine Johnson in the student paper, *The Aztec Press*, or in the arts periodical, *LitMag*. Nor, most tellingly, was she listed among the graduates in any subsequent year. It was likely she'd stayed a relatively short time, certainly a good deal less than the standard two years.

But what did strike him was the prominence at the time of a student named Graebler—*Allen* Graebler, with an extra 'e.' He was all over the place, the leader of numerous campus protests, regularly quoted in the student paper spouting revolutionary rhetoric. There were also lots of pictures, showing a good looking kid with long black hair and piercing eyes. Often he was at a microphone; and often too, he seemed to be surrounded by adoring women.

It was in going through these, aided by a magnifying glass, that Danny spotted Francine. The photo was captioned *OJC Students Demand Racial Justice, Gender Liberation, Free Tuition*, and she was among the throng to the right of the charismatic Graebler, at the podium. The shot nicely captured the passion of that chaotic era, the students caught in mid-chant, fists in the air and fire in their young eyes. A large banner behind them read *HANDS OFF OUR BODIES AND OUR MINDS!*

"Oh, how lucky!" said the nice lady at the school's alumni office, scanning the list of graduates on her computer screen. "He's right here in town."

Not a huge surprise. There were aging Allen Graeblers hanging around college towns throughout America—guys in their 40s, 50s, 60s, still uniformed in denim, who could never quite depart the scene of the glory years.

Although the school had only a post office box on file for Graebler, Danny readily found him in the Tucson Business Directory as the proprietor of AEG Cabinetry and Design, with a Speedway Boulevard address.

Walking into the shop, he was hit by the powerful smell of sawdust and fresh varnish. There was no one in sight, so he began looking around. *Nice stuff*, he thought. Gorgeous stuff in fact. Finely wrought tables and cabinets, credenzas and sideboards with deft Mexican flourishes, Mission oak-style rockers. He was kneeling to closely examine a cabinet with strange, undulating ribs when Graebler emerged from the back.

"Hey," he said in greeting. "Didn't know anyone was here."

The youthful vigor had long since given way to a sort of post-hippie-era seediness. Though he was balding and what remained of his hair was streaked with grey, he still wore it long, in a ponytail, and his worn jeans were held in place by a colorful woven belt.

"Gorgeous stuff you got here. You make it all yourself?"

He nodded his appreciation. "I did."

"What's this wood, anyway?" asked Danny, indicating the cabinet.

"Saguaro."

"The cactus?"

"From the skeleton. Believe it or not, that stuff is hundreds of years old." He paused. "Looking for anything in particular?"

"No, just looking around. I'm from Texas." That part was true, anyhow. "Just in town checking out colleges for my daughter."

"U of A?"

"That'll be next. I was over at Oracle this morning."

"Oh, yeah? I went there."

"Really? How'd you like it?"

"Hey, man, it was a great time to be in college. Not that I'm using any of it." He checked his watch. "Listen, I don't mean to rush you, but I gotta grab some lunch."

"Oh, okay," Danny said, heading for the door.

"But, no problem, why don't you stay and look around, maybe you'll find something for your daughter." Then, noting Danny's surprise, "You gotta believe in people. That's one thing I still keep from back then."

"That's a nice life philosophy; the world could use more of it."

"Yeah... well, I try anyway."

"Maybe I'll just walk with you, if you don't mind. I'd love to hear more about the school."

"Sure. Why not?"

"Wherever she goes, I just want to make sure she's comfortable. Us being Mexican-American and all...."

"I hear you," he said meaningfully, closing the door without locking it. "Right on."

* * *

"Sounds like the place was a total blast back then," Danny said half an hour later, watching Graebler rip into a platter of baby backs at Famous Dave's.

"It was, man, it really was. Good times."

"So you guys really shook up the place," Danny said, loading up his burger with his usual helping of ketchup.

"We sure as hell did. All these conservative administrators, they didn't know what hit 'em. This was Arizona in the *'70s*, man. It was sex, drugs and rock'n roll all the time, not to mention politics. Total mayhem."

Danny smiled. "Sounds pretty good."

"Oh, man! You wouldn't think it seeing me now, but I used to get a lot of tail! A *lot.*"

Danny laughed. "I believe it."

"Lemme tell you." He leaned forward. "Man, the stories I could tell...."

"I'm all ears."

"You're not a spy for my wife, are you?" He laughed again, his eyes alive, seeming to be reliving those wondrous times already. He paused to call over the waitress. "Hey, Angie, can we get a couple more brews over here? We might be around a while."

The stories weren't much—little more than a running tally of his conquests—but he lingered lovingly over each name. There were Patricia and her roommate Allison, collaborators in a wondrous, month-long threesome; the two Susans, Susan T. and Susan W.; there was Margie, the redhead, who was later raped while hitchhiking; and Sam, who was also his English T.A.

"Wow!" Danny grinned. "Now *that's* how to do college."

"Tell me about it." Then, as if to establish that it was all true and real, not just the usual bullshit, he said, "Of course, these are women we're talking about. There were also some that were trouble."

"How do you mean?"

"Oh, you know, they just didn't get that I wasn't into anything long term. One girl, Barb, she got pregnant—twice!"

"Not good."

"Thought it'd get me to marry her. *Twice!* I swear, the second time, I thought she might actually have the kid. Scared the living shit outta me." He laughed, took a long sip of beer. "Then there was another one, Francine! Man, she was the worst of all."

Danny waited a moment. "Yeah?"

"We used to do a lot of politics together, me and her. I totally turned that girl around, radicalized her, and she really got into it. I mean, I was militant, man, but she was *angry* militant."

Danny gave him a confused look to show he didn't get it.

"I was all for sticking it to the man, you know, but this girl, she wanted to *destroy* stuff."

"How do you mean?"

"You know, break windows. Get it on with cops. I mean, *crazy.*" He paused. "'Course, that also made her dynamite in bed."

Danny chuckled.

"Thing is, after a while it was like she thought she owned me. If I even looked at another chick, she'd totally lose it. So finally, you know, I had to confront her on it, let her know it was uncool, and she had to give me my space. That was it. She started screaming and yelling, cursing me out, *beating on* me." He paused. "Here's the thing—I had this great car, a '62 Pontiac Tempest LeMans. And just a couple of days later, I'm on I-10, doing about eighty, and suddenly I throw a piston rod and blow the engine. Turns out there's no oil cause someone loosened the plug in the oil pan. Didn't exactly seem like a coincidence."

"Jesus! What'd you do?"

He gave a what-could-I-do shrug. "Nothing, man, she was gone. Turned out she'd dropped out of school and split, just went wherever she went." He smiled wistfully. "I really loved that car... guess I was paying for my sins."

"Never heard from her again?"

"Thank God. I did think about her, though, when I read about that guy that cheated on his wife and she sliced off his pecker."

Danny laughed along with him, even as he was thinking, *And Francine never forgot you either. Somewhere along the line, she took your name, like she'd already taken your politics.*

* * * * *

The founders of Chester College were Congregationalists, decent and principled men committed to the ideal of education leading to moral uplift. That's why, in 1874, when construction began, they saw to it that allusions to that noble mission were strategically placed on walls and entryways around the campus. They understood that times might change, and fashions, but the vital thing was that future generations of scholars never lose sight of that cherished legacy.

Unsurprisingly, the first such reminder—the words *We come in reverence, we pray for mankind*—was engraved on the stone archway leading to the college chapel, and for a century and more, through good times and bad, it greeted Chester students. Now, about to pass beneath it, Will noted that *reverence* had been replaced by *tolerance*, and *mankind* by *diversity*.

Beside him, Barbara Ann Doyle smiled at him. "Well, at least they still pray."

"So did the Aztecs... while committing human sacrifice."

They slipped into the back row. With its stained glass, vaulted arches and heavy oaken entryways, the building retained much of its neo-Gothic splendor, but it was the newer decorative elements that spoke to its current function. Multi-colored banners hanging from the ceiling celebrated liberation theology and COEXISTence. A mural along one wall showed children of many hues holding hands, while the one opposite was festooned with calls in multiple languages for understanding and social justice. And prominently displayed on either side of where the altar had once stood, there were now displayed the wiccan symbols for protection and rebirth.

Within minutes of their arrival, every seat was taken, and soon the aisles and doorways were also jammed. The place was a sea of orange and red, since almost everyone else—students, faculty, even visiting press—had followed to the letter the memo disseminated by the president's office, headed *Grief, Healing and Accountability* and which described those as *the colors of healing and renewal, as the Chinese have taught us*. Long accustomed to standing out in every crowd, in his black three-piece suit, Will had never been so conspicuous as he was today.

"Like your guts," Doyle remarked.

"Yours too," he said, for she was in jeans and a blue work shirt. "Nah, she said, lifting the shirt to reveal a burnt off-brown belt that more or less passed muster. "Totally wimped out." She smiled, nodding at Bennett a few rows down and on the aisle. "Of course, not as bad as some."

Will glanced his brother's way. He was wearing fire-engine red pants and a polyester jacket mismatched by several shades.

"Where the hell did he come up with that get-up, anyway?" she laughed, "Bozo have a yard sale?" But catching Will's look, she regretted it. "Sorry, that was over the top."

"No problem. What's really sad is he actually had that stuff in his closet."

Now it was Will's turn to feel a twinge of remorse. After all, Bennett was under terrible stress, every aspect of his future uncertain. So who could really blame him for hoping a jacket and pair of pants might help placate the bastards? Meanwhile, here he was, cracking wise with the woman Bennett held responsible for destroying his life. "Bennett's not a bad guy," he allowed. "You gotta get to know him."

"Yeah, I know."

Still, a moment later, Will couldn't resist. "I've really gotta get Laura out of your clutches." He looked again at his brother's get-up. "I mean, look at him; he'll *never* get anyone else." He laughed, then admonishingly slapped himself on the cheek. "Shut up, Will."

Now a boy and girl—he with waist-length hair and holding a guitar, she, close cropped, in a red jump suit—padded their way to the front, positioning themselves between the wiccan symbols. Without preamble, he began strumming, and she sang. The song was "Hurt," Johnny Cash's cover of the Nine Inch Nails' mournful dirge about impending death, and to Will's surprise they weren't half-bad. They brought to the song almost as much conviction as the bitter and disillusioned Cash.

I hurt myself today
To see if I still feel.
I focus on the pain
The only thing that's real.

The next song, the Pernice Brothers' "Chicken Wire," grabbed the crowd even more. Its protagonist was a woman committing suicide inside her car, and for almost everyone, it uncannily evoked the symbolic death—the death of innocence—they'd just suffered right here at Chester.

She'd come so far to end her life,
By the rusty mower and chicken wire
By the chicken wire and studded tire
By the rusty mower and chicken wire

The musicians silently walked off to muted sobs and a few blown noses. They were replaced by a large figure with a shaved head and a flowing saffron robe, and it was only when she spoke that Will discerned she was a woman.

"Can a woman be a Buddhist monk?" whispered Will.

"That's Dr. Barber," Doyle replied *soto vocce*. "Runs the Counseling Center. I used to go out with her."

Will's eyes widened in surprise.

"Lousy in bed."

Up front, Dr. Barber was already exhorting the audience. "Go ahead, weep. Weeping is okay here! Weeping is healthy! Weeping is sanity!"

She cocked her hand to her ear—and from all sides came the sobs, in unembarrassed profusion. "More!" she enthused. "*More!* It feels so good, doesn't it?" Then, spreading her arms wide, she proclaimed, "Yes! We weep together, in pain and solidarity! We weep because we are wounded! We weep because we are scared! We weep because otherwise we must mourn!"

Will raised an eyebrow. "I don't get it. What does that mean?"

"That's 'cause you don't spend enough time around here."

"It is scary being scared," continued Dr. Barber, in a softer voice. "Unfortunately, I cannot tell you not to be—not after what we have all experienced. Not when we never know who's out there, waiting. Waiting around the next corner, or even in the dorm room down the hall." She paused. "This is why I promise you, in this sacred place, that we at the Counseling Center will always be there for you. Classes may be suspended, but the Counseling Center will remain open 24/7, three hundred and sixty-five days a year! We are always there, so we can be scared as one, in togetherness!"

With a flourish, Dr. Barber swept off to the side. There was a momentary silence, and then Dr. Frank, Chester's president, rose from his seat in the front pew to take her place. He surveyed the audience a long moment. "I love you all. At this moment I feel that more strongly than I ever have."

"We love you!" a lone voice answered back.

He nodded. "I know you do. And I also know how much you love this institution, with its long tradition of positive human interaction." He paused. "You came here to learn, and what you have learned here at Chester is far more important than anything to be found by reading books or sitting in classrooms. You've received an education in *being human.* You've learned what it means to *stand up* against those who would deny the precious humanity of others!"

Despite himself, Will had to acknowledge that the guy's delivery was better than that of a lot of the assholes he faced off against in court. Already he had the room in the palm of his hand. Even his brother was leaning forward, rapt.

"But lately we have learned something new and terrible: that there are some within our very own community who are full of bigotry and hate. And, yes, one of our most beloved own has suffered the awful consequences."

He paused dramatically, then thrust his arm toward the closed door on the side. "My friends, the bravest person I know!"

The instant Francine Grabler walked through the door, the place erupted. Draped in a fire engine red muu muu, she walked haltingly, obviously not fully recovered from her ordeal, and Frank rushed over to help ease her to the front. When she got there, the crowd rose as a body with a joyous roar. Grabler stood with uplifted face, modest and radiant, as the sound showered down upon her.

At last President Frank raised his hands, and the noise began to subside. "Francine, we all know how hard it is for you to be here today," he said. "You are our inspiration!"

This was met with another roar.

"Difficult as it is, might you be able to say a few words?"

She hesitated, shook her head, and for a moment it seemed she simply couldn't. Then, barely above a whisper: "Such terrible cruelty... so many bullies. It is hard to go on."

There was a moment of respectful silence, broken when someone yelled, "You must! You must!"

Others immediately took up the call, as Grabler watched with a sad, grateful smile.

"I love you all," she whispered. "Just, please, *please* stop the hate."

This set off the familiar chant. "Stop the hate! Stop the hate! Stop the hate!"

Though she was too weak to join in, her head bobbed to the rhythm. It went on until President Frank, arm around her shoulder, quieted the crowd.

"Yes, we will," he said firmly. "We *will* stop the hate. I promise you, here and now, we *will* find the haters. They *will* be rooted from our community."

Will locked eyes with Doyle. No words were necessary.

"Stop the hate," Frank intoned once more. "That is *my personal mission*. Because until that happens, there will be no healing!"

* * * * *

The article in *The New York Times*, headlined *One College's Crusade Against Intolerance*, appeared two days later on page A7, and ran two columns to the bottom of the page. It was accompanied by a photo of Warren Frank in a bow tie. It had been taken a good number of years before, and had been given to the paper of record by Chester's PR arm, aka The Office of Public Affairs and Interpersonal Understanding. In it, he appeared both earnest and appealingly human.

From the look of it, it seemed the Chester's PR people might also have written the story:

> At a time when colleges and universities across the country are struggling with the volatile issue of campus intolerance, one elite institution is taking the sort of aggressive action that might well serve as a model for the rest. In the aftermath of what local police describe as "a shocking hate crime," apparently aimed at silencing a professor known nationally as a crusader for victims' rights, Chester

College President Warren A. Frank has pledged "the harshest possible measures" against those deemed responsible for creating the climate that led to the incident. He has pointedly failed to exclude students and even faculty from those potentially subject to such sanction.

"We find ourselves in a situation where we just have to say, Enough!" President Frank explained in an interview, describing the attack, which defaced the residence of Professor Francine Grabler with ethnic and anti-women slurs, as "beyond anything I'd imagined possible at Chester." Obviously distraught as he clutched a throw pillow emblazoned with the college seal, he added, "We've had enough of giving free rein to haters. Free speech is one thing, and naturally we cherish it. But our highest priority must always be the physical and emotional safety of our community. That alone can lead to the healing we all seek."

At an emotional gathering of the Chester community Tuesday, Mr. Frank spoke of a subculture "that promotes bigotry and hatred" at the school, indicating that he was prepared to take all steps necessary to end it. Elaborating yesterday, he stressed that no one on campus was exempt from scrutiny, noting that school administrators and reliable faculty were reviewing the records of a number of individuals. He added pointedly that "though haters generally come in only one color, they are of all sizes and shapes and ages. Nor do they necessarily wear hoods or carry signs against a woman's right to choose; some may even be found in college classrooms—sometimes even at the front."

He said that if any faculty members were determined to have been involved in promoting the atmosphere that led to the attack, they would face suspension or even termination, as would those students deemed to have "fallen under their sway."

Dr. Grabler, the target of the attack, is the school's Distinguished Professor of Victim Studies. She has written extensively in her field, been much honored for her pioneering work, and has lately been said to be under consideration for a top post in the Department of Education.

At Chester, Professor Grabler has made the fight against intolerance into a personal crusade, and as a result has found herself in conflict with a number of older and more conservative faculty, notably in the sciences. Sources at the school report that her primary antagonist has been Dr. Alexander Kane, an Arkansas-born ex-Marine who teaches Electrical Engineering.

Dr. Kane declined to be interviewed, but in a statement issued through his lawyer, Jacob Paul, he asserted he had "done nothing wrong to or regarding Ms. Grabler. My only interest is, and has been, protecting the integrity of my department."

While Mr. Frank has yet to reveal evidence specifically linking Dr. Kane or any other individual to the attack, he claims "personal knowledge of a direct threat of physical violence made against Professor Grabler."

The article continued for another few hundred words, going into Chester's history, as well as citing episodes of intolerance at a number of other schools around the country.

Will, who had been reading the article aloud to Bennett, set aside the paper with a sigh. After a few seconds he picked it up again to study Frank's photo. "Just look at that smug prick! What is it they say about generals? From time to time you have to hang one, as an example to the others? Same goes for college presidents." He jerked his head in the general direction of the campus. "On a lamppost, right on the fucking quad! You got a pen?"

A shell-shocked Bennett handed him one. "What do we do now, Will?"

Distractedly, Will began drawing a Hitler moustache on the photo. "You got a number for this guy Kane? I say it's about time we consolidated our forces."

* * * * *

It was the damnedest thing—Danny had never seen anything like it. After Tucson, the Francine Johnson trail went stone cold. Pfffft. She had simply disappeared—not to resurface until nearly eight years later, under her borrowed name, as an author/activist.

Of course, there was her official bio. According to that, she earned both her undergraduate and graduate degrees at University of Texas, and obviously these were the years when she'd have done it. Yet four days of poking around the Austin campus proved a reprise of the Tucson experience. No record of her anywhere. No Francine Johnson or Grabler listed among the graduates.

No telephone listing for those years. No mention of her either in school or local periodicals. Nothing.

He considered other angles. Might she have attended under yet another name? Perhaps having married in the interim? He couldn't completely dismiss the possibility. Yet how, he had to wonder, had someone with her academic record—lousy high school grades, junior college drop-out—been admitted to so prestigious a university under any circumstances? Had she perhaps submitted a phony transcript? He'd seen that trick pulled off before, and by individuals less devious than Francine Grabler, and seeking admission to top colleges far smaller, and thus likely far more vigilant, than the 50,000-student behemoth U of T.

In short, Danny found himself something he didn't like to be: flummoxed. This case was unlike any he'd ever pursued. This woman was not simply elusive, she was positively chameleon-like.

When Francine did initially reappear as Grabler, it was not in the flesh, but simply by name on the cover of a book, as the co-author (with one Melissa Leary) of *I Am My Own Father, Mother and Best Friend*. It was published by Outta Sight Books, and the cover illustration was a black and white abstract of a woman screaming in anguish. Yet even then, there appeared no photo of either author on the jacket.

In fact, based on his preliminary inquiries, Melissa Leary was proving as hard to run down as the young Johnson/Grabler.

He learned, not at all to his surprise, that Outta Sight Books had been defunct since the late '80s. Its back-listed books had then been taken over by Copasetic Press; which in turn had been swallowed up by Five Finger

Discount Media; which in the course of time, was itself subsumed by Random House, part of the multi-national Bertelsmann conglomerate.

Thus it was that, deciding to make a quick stop in New York, Danny found himself on the 34th floor of a glass office tower on East 50th Street, giving the young receptionist his most winning smile.

It wasn't working.

"Look," he said. "I'm just looking to contact one of your authors."

"I'm sorry," she said, not sorry at all. "We don't give out that information."

"It's extremely important; I wouldn't ask otherwise."

"I suggest you write, requesting that information."

"To whom would I write? Do you have a name?"

She gazed at him with disinterest. "Someone in rights and permissions."

"Do you have a name?"

"Excuse me?"

"Could you tell me who that might be?"

She sighed and picked up her laminated list. "Ms. Marvin."

"Good. Thank you." He paused. "Could you call her for me? Right now?"

"I told you, Sir, we are not authorized—"

"I'll give you a hundred dollars."

That stopped her. "Pardon me?"

He reached into his jacket pocket. "I've got it right here." In fact, knowing how pathetically little the Ivy-League educated underlings at these places got paid for the privilege of working in this snotty business, he'd come prepared with ten crisp C-notes, but if he was about to shortchange anyone, she was it.

She hesitated. "Really?"

He snapped it in front of her face. "Right here in my clammy little hands. Just tell her there's a really nice guy here in the reception area who needs to see her. You can even say he's really good looking."

Several minutes later, Ms. Marvin, all 250-plus pounds of her, lumbered into the reception area, confusion on her face. Danny rose to meet her, smiling, hand extended. "Ms. Marvin?"

"Yes?"

"My name's Jeffrey Rivera. I know this is unorthodox, but I'm very eager to get in touch with one of your authors."

"I'm awfully sorry," she said sympathetically, "but I'm not allowed."

"I understand that," he nodded. "But I'm hoping these are special circumstances."

"Who, exactly, are you trying to contact?"

"Her name in Melissa Leary."

If the name registered, it was only dimly.

"Are you familiar with Francine Grabler?"

Her face lit up like Times Square. "Francine Grabler? Ohmygod, are you kidding? I *love* her work!"

"Me too! Leary was her earliest collaborator."

"*Pain and Anguish...* I read it for my favorite women's studies class at Harvard. I never had any book speak to me so personally, it explained so much!"

"I hear you!" He smiled broadly, shaking his head at the depth of their common bond. "Listen, if you have a few minutes, can I buy you a cup of coffee?"

* * *

Danny already had a pretty good idea he'd be able to hold onto the rest of the cash, and by the time Gretchen Marvin had demolished her first piece of cherry pie, he was certain. "Omygod!" she was saying. "I could hardly believe what those fascist bastards did to Francine up at Chester! It made me physically ill!"

"Me too!"

"Did you read the piece in *The Times*? They didn't give Francine nearly enough credit for all she's done!"

"I know. That's what I want to do with this piece I'm writing, really get into depth about her work and her history."

"Good!" she agreed decisively. "Who'd you say it's for?"

"I didn't." He made like he was slightly flustered. "I'm a freelancer. I'm hoping to place it in *The Nation*."

"Omygod, that'd be perfect!"

"Or maybe even *The New York Review of Books*." He smiled modestly. "A guy can dream, can't he?"

"Either one would be great!"

"I'm not kidding myself; it won't be easy," he allowed, bringing his accent up half a notch, allowing for the possibility, however farfetched, that even at these bastions of progressivism, his ethnicity just might be something editors held against him. "That's why I'm here. I want to research the hell out of this thing—"

"I *really* look forward to reading it."

"Because no subject could be more important to me."

"But, you know, like I say, I'm really not supposed to give out that information. A lot of our authors are extremely protective of their privacy."

He nodded his understanding, thinking, *Is it really going to come to that? Am I actually going to have to sleep with her?*

She looked at him earnestly. "Can't you just get in touch with Francine up at Chester?"

"I know, I intend to—or rather, *hope* to. If she'll talk to me."

She smiled.

"But I want to do all the research first, show her how serious I am about this. Besides, I know she's hurting right now."

"I understand. I'd be so intimidated meeting her myself."

"Have you read *I Am My Own Father....*"

"*Mother and Best Friend!* Ohmygod, of course!"

"So if Melissa Leary would talk to me it would be really special. I've never read an interview with her anywhere."

"It's true, I certainly haven't heard much about her. She's completely disappeared, hasn't she?"

"She has. So here I am. you're my last hope." He smiled. "Make that my *only* hope."

She leaned across the table and winked. "Let's see what I can do. Our secret."

* * * * *

"Good Christ almighty!" said Alexander Kane, studying a photo of Grabler's defaced wall. "So much fuss over *this*?"

Having deliberately avoided venturing anywhere near the crime scene—and the naked hostility he was sure to draw if he did—it was only now, flipping through photos in Bennett Tripp's living room, that Kane was seeing the scrawled words that were likely to cost him his career. He looked up from the close up of *BITCH-Liar* and grinned. "I don't get it—it's not like it isn't true."

"Hey," came a sharp caution from his lawyer, sitting beside him on the couch. "You can't be caught talking that way, so stop *thinking* that way."

Already, ten minutes into this meeting to set strategy, Will had formed a pretty definite opinion of both Kane and his lawyer. Kane, in neatly pressed slacks and a classic blue blazer, was precisely as advertised: a gentleman of the old school, almost courtly with his lilting Arkansas accent, but rock solid at the core. Clearly it was no accident he had landed in this fix, and he was facing it with calm fortitude, and more, the sense he wouldn't have done anything differently.

On the other hand, there was the lawyer, Jason Paul of the white shoe New York firm of Anson, Larsen and Hart, whom Kane had hired on the recommendation of a well-meaning friend. Even before the meeting, Will had pegged him as a jerk, knowing that Paul did work on the side for the world's whiners and cause-aholics, including the ACLU, those loathsome defenders of the indefensible always worshipfully described by media pansies as "the nation's most venerable rights organization." Sure enough, within seconds he let it drop that he'd leapt at taking on this case not because he agreed with his client's worldview—he pointedly did not—but because it looked to be a solid First Amendment case.

More, Paul looked the part—40-ish, hair just so, stylish suit from Italy or some damn place, designer glasses that would've covered the rent on Will's apartment but still failed to hide his too-moist eyes—a classic wimp.

Personal feelings aside, this was not good for their common cause. If there was to be any hope of winning this case, he needed street brawlers on his side. God knows their adversaries weren't about to pull any punches. Already, pending the conclusion of an investigation of the episode by a school panel packed with Grabler's faculty allies, all the signers of Kane's petition had been put on notice that they were facing suspension, and handwriting experts were working to determine the identities of the *anonymous* signers. Too, there was talk that all Electrical Engineering majors would be made to attend special sensitivity training classes, so as not to be permanently warped by exposure to unhealthy ideological thoughts. Kane's two student assistants, Sergei and Than, were in particular jeopardy, facing the very real possibility of expulsion for having circulated the damning document.

As if all that wasn't bad enough, the two other faculty members who'd signed their names to the petition had already apologized, not only acknowledging their guilt but pledging to accept without challenge whatever punishment was finally meted out.

Kane drew a pack of Marlboros from his pocket. "Lousy habit, but doesn't seem quite the right time to give it up."

"I wish you wouldn't," Paul said, looking to Will and Bennett for support. "Breathing in toxic fumes isn't my idea of fun." He smiled, making like he was an okay guy. "Unless we're talking cannabis, of course."

Bennett spoke up sharply. "Know what? It's my house and I've got no problem with it!"

Will looked at his brother, perched at the edge of the other chair facing the couch, and smiled inwardly.

Bennett was the one huge surprise to come out of this mess! At last, all of Will's haranguing and belittling was starting to pay dividends. In the face of impending disaster, knowing he'd soon be identified as one of "the Anonymous Four," as campus terminology had it, not only had he stopped whining, he was getting *angry*. He'd informed his brother that if he had to go down, he'd go down at Will's side, fighting.

Here was the brother Will had long craved and hoped against hope was inside the lily-livered academic he loved anyway. Now, thinking optimistically, he figured even if Bennett was out of a job with no prospects, at least his new attitude might get him laid.

"That's all right, Son," Kane said, pocketing the cigarettes. "Not that I don't appreciate it."

"Well, let me at least get you something to drink, Dr. Kane," Bennett said, rising. "Beer, wine, bourbon?"

"Beer'll be fine. And the name's Alex."

"Right." Then, pointedly looked at Paul. "*Alcohol's* allowed, I hope."

"Of course," Paul said.

"The carpet's also mine," Bennett said, "so if anyone feels the need to puke on it, feel free!"

Ah, Will thought proudly, for he had seen the phenomenon before, *nothing like the zeal of he with a newly grown pair!* Bizarre and awkward as Bennett's performance was, his brother found it touching. Bennett was so ashamed of his earlier readiness to leave his new comrade in arms in the lurch that he was determined now to leave no doubt as to his loyalty.

Until now, the professor of Electrical Engineering had dealt with Bennett only in passing, and he looked at his physics colleague with bemusement. "That's quite an invitation, but I think I can handle one beer."

Will clapped his hands. "All right, then. Now, Dr. Kane, before we get to your dealings with—" He couldn't bring himself to say the name. "This woman—"

"Professor Grabler," Paul said, helpfully.

"Yes, *her*... could you fill me in a bit on your background?"

Kane waited a moment for Bennett to set out the beers and resume his seat. "Well, it's a pretty straightforward tale. I grew up in Ft. Smith, Arkansas, not much of a student, so right outta high school I went into the military. This was '68, so that meant 'Nam. Stayed in the next twenty-three years, and left as a lieutenant colonel. Then I came here."

"So that's where you began your training in electronics, in the military?"

"Right. I started in the infantry. I was a sniper, actually."

"A sniper?" Paul sounded distressed. "Did you ever actually kill a person?

"No, I wouldn't say so."

"Well, that's a relief."

"But I killed a lot of the enemy."

Will laughed.

Bennett noted Paul's distress. "Some people are so politically correct, they'd like battlefields to be handicap-accessed."

Will looked at his brother in surprise. He'd seen the line on the Internet and repeated it to Bennett, but he was more than pleased to have him appropriate it for his own purposes.

Kane nodded, and continued. "The military gave me everything. A career, a college education, everything. That's how I began in electronics. After the war, I stayed in, specializing in explosives. I got my Ph.D. when I got out, and they hired me here as an assistant professor. That's about it." He paused, then added, unnecessarily. "It was a different place then."

"And how'd this trouble with Grabler start?" asked Will.

"Listen, if it was up to me, I'd never have had anything to do with the woman. She knows diddly about what I do, and I don't give a good half damn about that nonsense of hers. Far as I'm concerned, this life's hard enough without wasting your time on lunatics."

Paul said, "Excuse me, but like it or not, Professor Grabler is a widely respected—"

"Lunatic!" Kane cut him off. "A highly respected *lunatic.*" He gave him a withering stare. "It was her that started all this. How the hell does that... I don't even wanna say the word... how does *she* tell *me* who we get to hire in my department? What, now we're supposed to hire people by their sex or skin color instead of what's between their ears?"

Will couldn't help but notice that with anger, Kane's accent grew heavier.

"You're not saying you're opposed to diversity?" asked Paul, as if scarcely able to process what he'd just heard.

"I'm sayin' it's my job to give my kids the best training possible, and that ain't the way to do it!"

"Let's be completely honest, Dr. Kane—wasn't her antagonism brought about by your attacks on the

Oppression Studies Center? Isn't that what started the whole thing?"

"Damn right! And not just because it'd mean $100 million down the toilet that a lot of other departments could use. Mine for instance! Christ, have you seen the plans they got for that place? I swear to God, some cooling system based on termite mounds in Africa that'll supposedly suck in only air with the right temperature, drinking fountains spouting recycled human piss, doodads attached to plants that'll let the damn plants *tell* you when they want a drink!" He looked closely at his lawyer; then, as if explaining to a mentally deficient child, he said, "Christ, man, I'm *fightin'* for this place! Is it gonna be a great school or just another wuss factory?" He stopped again. "Damn right I said some harsh things about the Oppression Studies Center. Know why? 'Cause they're *true*. But maybe that's not a good enough reason anymore."

Paul seemed hardly to have heard. "You're telling me you have no regrets?"

"Did I say that? I regret that my kids are havin' to pay the price!"

Will and Bennett nodded their agreement, but his lawyer only stared at him impassively.

There was a long silence.

"Well, let me ask you directly," Paul finally said, "who else do you think might've done it? Because, like it or not, that's the question everyone's asking. Can you think of anyone else around here with as much against her as you?"

"Lots of people!" snapped Kane. "Anyone with half a brain and a skull to put it in! The woman's a menace!"

"Finding that asshole's not our job, by the way," Will said. "Our job is just showing that these guys had nothing to do with it. And in that regard, they've got nothing. Zilch. It's laughable. There's no evidence at all linking you guys to what happened." He paused. "Listen, supposedly everything that happens around here is on surveillance tapes, right? Know what I get when I press campus security on that? First they tell me the cameras were down, then they tell me that the house is officially off campus, so it wasn't covered. I've never been anyplace where they manufacture so much high-grade bullshit! You think any of that's gonna stand up in any court of law?"

They continued talking for another half-hour, with Will systematically laying waste to whatever case the other side might pretend to have. But of course, he had no ready answer to the question that hung heavily in the air: *Will the facts even remotely matter?*

Not that the meeting didn't result in some important progress. As Kane was on his way out, bending toward Will at the door to shake his hand, he whispered, "From here on in, you're my lawyer too. I don't care if you gotta file a damn restraining order, I don't want that sanctimonious jackass anywhere near me!"

* * * * *

Hey, Danny reasoned, this was Greenwich, Connecticut, one of the toniest little burgs in this great land, and he needed to fit in, didn't he? How better than in a Mercedes BMG M5 rental, courtesy of Marty Katz? It's not like he'd sprung for a Rolls or a Ferrari. Besides, in the event he had to make a quick escape—admittedly, highly unlikely, but you never knew—with its M1 engine capable of producing speeds of 150 mph, this little baby was the fastest production sedan in the world.

Then there was the interior. Reclining in the driver's seat, eyes half-closed as he listened to Howard Stern on Serius XM, the smell of the leather was almost erotic.

By now he'd been waiting here on Lawrence Lane in this enclave of impossibly expensive homes for more than two hours, and he was so caught up in his reverie that it took him a moment to respond to the sight of the woman emerging from the imposing Tudor several doors down. Well dressed and looking to be in her mid-'70s, she nonetheless moved briskly as she made for the Lincoln Navigator by the garage. Danny watched it head down the long, sloping drive onto the street, then waited four slow beats, and followed.

She led him past still more blocks of multi-million dollar properties, each fronted by a vast, manicured lawn, then turned onto Greenwich Avenue, the town's main shopping drag, lined with upscale clothing shops and pricey eateries. She drove the Navigator into a spot and Danny, keeping an eye on his prey in the rear view, took one farther down the block.

He watched her window shop for a few minutes, noting that she kept an eye on her watch, before she entered a French-style bakery/café called Avignon. He strolled in a couple of minutes later and ordered a cappuccino at the counter. By then the woman was sitting a small table in the corner, talking animatedly with her lunch date, another woman of about the same age.

He was outside, leaning against his car, when they emerged from the café, and he watched as they lingered a few moments more on the sidewalk, then exchanged a quick embrace and air kisses and headed off in opposite directions.

She passed within five feet of him and, up close, he saw that she had the dignified, old-moneyed air of so many around here, her fine grey head nicely set off by a forest green silk scarf.

He began casually following, then called, "Excuse me, Miss?"

Striding purposefully, oblivious, she didn't respond.

"Melissa Leary?"

It was several steps before she slowed, stopped, turned. When she did, her still-attractive face registered not just surprise, but apprehension. "Are you talking to me?"

Danny walked toward her. "I believe so," he said pleasantly.

"My name's Mayhew."

"Really?" he said.

"Jean Mayhew."

He of course already knew that, had learned it within an hour of getting the Lawrence Lane address from the sweet and trusting Ms. Marvin; as he also knew her husband, Russell, a retired investment banker, was currently undergoing treatment for prostate cancer.

"Oh, my mistake," he said, "So sorry to trouble you."

But—bingo!—rather than turn away, she lingered, distinctly uncomfortable. "Who are you? What do you want?"

"My name's Jeffrey Rivera. Actually, I'm researching an article on Francine Grabler."

Now, flashing in her eyes, came something unmistakably, like panic. "I have no idea who that is."

"She's a writer, quite famous. Melissa Leary, the woman I'm looking for, used to write with her. She's from here in Greenwich. I've been poking around, making inquiries, and someone referred me to you. I think she probably still lives here."

"Who?" she demanded.

He nodded vaguely behind. "Some guy back there, in the French bakery." A stretch, to be sure, but not entirely implausible. He'd long ago learned that what they say about small towns applies even to wealthy ones: there are precious few secrets, and almost anyone is likely to know, or at least suspect, something about anyone else. Anyway, if it threw her even further off balance, so much the better.

"Well, he was mistaken," she said adamantly. "Now, if you'll excuse me, I have errands to run!"

"Of course. And again, I apologize."

But he noted that instead of continuing down Greenwich Avenue, she returned immediately to her car and that, as she pulled out, she nearly hit a passing car.

* * *

With a sinking heart, Danny realized sacrifices would have to be made. Since he'd foolishly allowed himself to be seen alongside the Mercedes, he reluctantly traded it in for a Honda Civic.

It was the right move. Four days later, late on a Sunday morning, a middle aged woman, mid to late 50s, dressed in loose corduroys and a sweatshirt, showed up at the Mayhew house in a six-year old Chevy Impala. She stayed several hours, until mid-afternoon, and then took off. Danny followed her the thirty miles up I-95 to the Henry Mucci Highway, then off the Golden Hill exit toward the working class town of Bridgeport. She slowed before a small two-story house on Elizabeth Street in need of a paint job and pulled into the narrow drive.

* * * * *

Will awoke to an unpleasant surprise. On this, the very day he'd at last been able to schedule a meeting with President Frank to discuss his clients' fate, *The New York Times* had run a short editorial following up on their earlier article.

Entitled *Whose Freedom?* it urged Frank to do the right thing—difficult as doing the right thing can sometimes be—and permanently remove from the Chester College community those faculty members linked to this crime. While we respect all points of view, those who challenge such fundamental precepts as tolerance and diversity must be given no quarter. We hope that in his final ruling on the case, due any time, President Frank will have the courage to follow through on his powerful and oft-stated convictions.

Reading it early that morning, Will snatched up his phone. Twenty minutes later, Marjorie Spivak and Arthur XXX Perkins were in his office.

"I want you guys in there with me. Arthur, you got your hoodie?"

Arthur nodded reluctantly. "I think it's back in the closet."

"I think it's back in the closet, *Whitey*," Will snapped. "Get with the program. And, Marjorie, bring both the titanium wheelchair *and* those old-fashioned leg braces."

"The Theodore Roosevelt ones?"

"Right, good enough. Either way, at some point I'm probably gonna want you on your feet."

Just then, the door opened and Marty Katz appeared. "What's the big deal that I had to leave a flooded basement on 79th Street?"

"Marty, I'm gonna need you to be a transvestite."

"Fuck that!"

"Just for maybe half an hour."

"Not even for half a second."

"I could loan you a dress," volunteered Marjorie.

Will ignored her. "We're going up to Chester to stick it to that bastard Frank. You can't come otherwise."

"No way, I'm definitely coming."

"Then be a man and say yes to the dress."

He nodded toward Marjorie. "She coming?"

"Absolutely."

"I'll push her chair."

"Not good enough," Will said, moving into negotiation mode. "All right, you can be gay and a recent victim of a hate crime."

"Huh uh, forget it."

"You don't have to come, you know." He sighed. "Okay, bi—nothing wrong with that."

"I'll be a victim," offered Katz, no slouch at negotiation himself, "but with the other part ambiguous. Christ, it's not like a straight person can't also get the shit beaten outta him in this town. And even gay bashers make mistakes."

Will agreed to that, with the stipulation, (after checking out the matter on the Internet), that his friend wear a pair of ass-emphasizing Ambercrombie and Ruehl khakis in a slim, low rise, boot-cut.

"Now, then," he said, turning to Arthur, "where the hell's that damn Redskin?"

* * *

The meeting was scheduled for 4:00, and The Dream Team showed up on the dot: Will, followed by Margaret, wobbling on her braces; then Arthur; then Marty Katz, a bloody patch on his forehead and pushing the empty wheelchair, the pants lending his step an unmistakable mince despite his best efforts; all of them trailed by a reeling Larry Harris, stinking of whiskey.

Will had to hand it to Frank, he hardly batted an eye, showing just a momentary flicker of alarm when the Indian missed the chair and landed sprawling on the century old Tabriz Carpet, in the process nearly upsetting a three million dollar Quing vase.

"Whoopsie daisy," Will said. Then, to Frank, with a knowing nod. "Native American."

"Of course, of course."

Will couldn't help but notice that on the president's desk was a pile of that day's *New York Times*, the one on top folded back to the editorial, with key phrases underlined.

"Glad you were able to fit us in," he offered with barely concealed scorn, looking to set a no-nonsense tone.

"Well, you seem like a...." He searched for the word. "Thoughtful group. And I expect you're as interested in a healing resolution to all this as I am."

Will glanced Arthur's way and gave a subtle nod.

"Shut up, Whitey," he said, though barely audibly.

"I understand," Frank said with a look of real concern. "This *is* a place of white privilege. What's your name, young man?"

"Arthur."

"Arthur *Three-X*," added Will. "A very able attorney, not to be trifled with."

"I don't doubt it."

"As we all are."

Will slid off his chair and stalked over to Frank's desk. "Let's get right down to it. This is nothing more than a simple case of vandalism that—"

"Vandalism?" he said, startled. "Were... were *lynchings* vandalism?"

"And we both know there is no evidence at all against my clients, not a scintilla, that even *begins* to justify the kinds of harsh penalties under consideration. I'm ready to prove they were nowhere near Professor Grabler's home on the night that this attack—"

"But don't you see," Frank said, this time throwing out his arms in sweet reason, "that can't be our only concern. Climate—climate change, if you will—that is the issue. We cannot allow hate to fester here at Chester. Until that fundamental concern is addressed, there can be no true healing."

"Are you telling me they're going to be fired?" Will demanded.

"I of course understand your distress, since one of the perpetrators is your brother," Frank allowed sympathetically. "But I'd hope that as a little person—" His sweeping gaze took in the others. "That all of you, as persons who've experienced the anguish and pain of harassment and exclusion, would join me in celebrating such a resolution. Because, as you know—"

"*Celebrate* it?" Will snapped, incredulous.

"As you know," Frank continued more firmly, tapping a finger on the editorial pile, "I am well known for my oft-stated principles."

Will tried another tact. "You speak of victims. Well, our clients too are victims."

Frank looked at him with a furrowed brow. "Really?" he asked, genuinely surprised. "How so?"

"They have been unjustly accused of a heinous crime, and punished on the basis of no discernible evidence."

Frank leaned back in his chair and clasped his hands behind his head, considering this. "Yes," he decided after a long moment, "I believe I can see where you are going with this. But you see, as a scholar I am concerned with specificity."

"Excuse me?"

He immediately regretted it, for already Frank was on his feet heading for the bookshelf. "Let me explain."

It took him only a moment to find what he was looking for. He handed the book to Harris. "You, my Native American friend, will especially appreciate this. It's by Dagmar Engstrom, an adjunct here in Victim Studies."

The Indian stared at the book in seeming incomprehension, and for a moment, Will wasn't sure he could read. But then he spoke haltingly, slurring the words. "Custer was no victim, his killers were."

"You see, language is a weapon!" exclaimed Frank. "It is appropriated by the powerful to subjugate the less powerful. By definition, a white male can *never* be a victim." He looked at his guests, immensely pleased with himself. "That is one of our jobs here at Chester, and one of the things I'm proudest of—our role in returning language, in this case victimhood, to its rightful owners." He nodded at Harris. "Like you."

"Are you really saying Professor Kane and my brother can't ever be in the right?"

"A male person of no-color can certainly experience physical pain," he allowed generously, "all the best research confirms that. And by owning up to his role in the oppression of others, he can eventually start to heal. But is that the same as being in the right? I fear not."

When no one responded, he smiled in satisfaction. "You see—you're getting the benefit of a $250,000 Chester education free of charge."

Will waited a moment. "I was hoping I wouldn't have to do this." He reached toward Marjorie, who handed him an envelope. He withdrew a sheet of paper and studied it a moment. "I've said there's no evidence in this case, but that's not quite right. In fact, there is evidence—evidence that Distinguished Professor Francine Grabler never received the degrees she claimed when she was hired by this institution."

This was a bluff, of course—a hopeful surmise based on the information Danny had so far passed on, but that's what desperation can do.

It didn't work. "How dare you, Sir?" Frank exploded. "How *dare* you! Among my oft-stated principles is a belief in justice, not in accusations without hard and fast proof!" He paused, staring angrily down at Will, who, though he stared back in defiance, remained silent, betraying the hollowness of his case.

"By the way," Frank said, "Dr. Grabler has more real experience, *life* experience, in her little finger—" He was so indignant he had to stop. "How *dare* you! Do you really think we're that elitist here, so invested in privilege? For your information, we currently have on our adjunct faculty, teaching our graduate course in Parenthood as Pathology, a welfare mother with nothing more than an elementary school equivalency certificate. And I hired her *personally*."

"Let's cut the bullshit! Why don't I just write you a check?"

Will turned to Katz in alarm. He was freelancing here. Although Will had already vetoed the idea, his landlord friend was instinctively falling back on what came naturally from his dealings with New York City bureaucrats. He also knew that Katz had probably hidden a recording device somewhere to get the goods on the bastard.

But the suggestion stopped Frank in his tracks, seeming to catch his interest.

"A hundred thousand bucks," Katz added meaningfully.

Frank gave a dismissive laugh and the moment passed; to the president of a highly ranked college, so modest a sum wasn't so much chicken feed as dog shit.

"Forgive my colleague," Will said lamely. "He's the recent victim of a savage beating."

"Of course," allowed Frank, well positioned to be magnanimous. With a smile he turned back to Larry Harris. "I'm eager to hear more from you, my friend."

Harris was staring with bleary-eyed hatred at his longtime foe, Katz, stunned at the figure he'd just thrown out. "Liar! So much for white man, peanuts for Indian!" he muttered. "Treaty breaker!"

"I know," agreed Frank sadly. "Every one of us who wasn't here before Columbus. What tribe are your people from, Son?"

"I want my land back."

"Of course you do."

"Or at least a two bedroom apartment."

Deeply impressed by his passion, Frank nodded his understanding. "I'm wondering...." he hesitated. "Just a thought. We've been looking around here for someone of your... stature. Might you be interested in an adjunct professorship?"

* * * * *

When Danny knocked on the door of the Elizabeth Street house early the next morning and asked for Melissa Leary, the woman before him stared at him fixedly for a moment. Clearly, she was not surprised.

"My name's Martha Mayhew," she said coolly. "I haven't gone by Melissa for a long time."

"Oh, I see."

With uncombed hair and careworn eyes, she seemed to be wearing the same clothes as yesterday.

"My mother told me someone had been asking. But I'm afraid there's nothing I can do for you."

"I see," he said smiling. "So the other was only your pseudonym."

She didn't answer, and certainly didn't seem about to invite him in.

"I actually followed you from Greenwich," he admitted, buying time.

Her short, unexpected laugh held no mirth. "I don't know if I should be flattered or terrified."

"Well, see, I don't know if your mother told you—"

"She told me she was approached by some creepy guy, and you are."

"Well, see," he fell back on the familiar ruse, "this article I'm writing on Francine Grabler—"

"I get it," she cut him off, making it clear her mother had also told her that, "and I'm not interested. Sorry you went to all the trouble."

She started to close the door, but he stopped it with his foot.

"Move your foot, now!"

"Can I at least give you this?" he said, fumbling in his pocket for a card. Though it identified him as Jeffrey Rivera, it was c/o Valenzuela, his real name, and included his actual Bronx home address and cell number.

Grudgingly, she took it. "Now move your damn foot!"

"Please, Ms. Leary," he pleaded, "this is so important to me—"

"Mayhew...."

"I'm so sorry, Ms. Mayhew. If you could please just give me five minutes."

When this gave her an instant's pause, he seized the opening. "I'm not really a writer," he admitted, speaking hurriedly, exaggerating his accent for effect. "Not yet, anyway. I'm trying to get started. My wife... she thinks I'm crazy."

When this elicited a hint of a smile, he pressed ahead. "My real job, see, I read meters for Con Ed in New Rochelle." *Who the hell would ever invent that?* "But what I want, what I pray for, is to make my living writing." He looked at her with hope in his eyes. "Writing about things that matter, things I care about. I'm 37 and I have a four year old little girl, so it really is now or never."

From the way she was leaning slightly forward—a classic sympathy tell—the bullshit was clearly starting to go over.

"Listen, I don't know what I even have to tell you. I haven't had any contact with Francine in a long, long time... at least twenty years."

"I understand. But if you could just help me out with a little bit on how the two of you came to write that wonderful book—"

"Your wife is right, you *are* crazy... but I suppose I've got to admire your dedication." She paused. "As long as I'm not identified, by name or in any other way. I'll need an absolutely firm commitment on that."

As soon as they were inside her living room, facing each other on comfortable but mismatched chairs, she returned to the subject.

'You must understand, I am an extremely private person. What you want to talk about, that was a long time ago. Another life."

"I do, I understand," he said. "I promise, I'll respect that. I won't use your name. This will all be for—what do they call it?—deep background."

"All right, as long as that's clear." She nodded. "So you've got your five minutes. The clock is running."

"Wait, hold on," he said, smiling as he opened his bag to get out his pad. "Don't start yet."

Not that he took her at face value. Having overcome the first, most daunting obstacle, getting in, he was confident he could win her trust, knowing from long experience that once even the most reluctant interviewees get rolling—and no one could get them rolling like Danny—they were likely to start spewing. Not only would they get caught up in their recollections, but it was as if at some point they'd begin to feel an obligation to entertain him and justify his interest.

Sure enough, Martha—or Melissa, as he continued to think of her—soon proved an extreme example of the phenomenon. Not only was she positively eager to share but, even better, lacked the filter possessed by most people that keeps them from saying what probably ought not be said.

Ten minutes in—five minutes after he was supposed to have left—out of the blue, she posed a question. "So what was the look on my mother's face when you approached asking for me?"

"She seemed kind'a surprised."

"I'll bet. *Just* surprised?"

Danny tried to guess what she wanted to hear. "It was pretty clear she didn't want to talk to me."

"You *think?*" she said with a broad smile. "Here's what you have to know about my mother: she gives new dimension to the term *proper*. To her, the Women's Club of Greenwich is cutting edge. So she's not exactly pleased by how I've lived my life."

"I see. She doesn't get it."

"That's putting it lightly. Embarrassed. Ashamed. Those are probably more on target. But no, it's true, she doesn't get me. Never has. But as you see, I'm still the dutiful daughter, I still troop over there for lunch every Sunday."

Danny glanced around, taking in the second hand furniture, the shelves haphazardly crammed with books, the desk piled with papers, the general disarray. The home might've been that of a struggling, overworked grad student.

"Pretty different from Greenwich, I guess."

"Exactly," she said dryly. "Look, it's hard to blame them. They think I'm wasting my life. And they're probably right."

Abruptly, to Danny's surprise, there came sounds from the floor above, followed immediately by someone moving heavily down the stairs.

"My son," she said.

"Ah."

"Gregory!"

"Yeah!"

"Come meet Mr....."

"Rivera," he offered.

"Rivera!"

A face appeared around the corner. He was in his mid-twenties, handsome, but bleary-eyed, having just awakened. It was close to 10:00 on a Monday morning. "Hi," he said tonelessly.

"Nice to meet you."

"Where you going, Kiddo?"

"Out. Got stuff to do." He disappeared, the front door closing a moment later after him.

She paused a moment, looking troubled. "Something else they've never really gotten over. Coming back home with a baby—" She made air quotes. "Out of wedlock."

For once, Danny was nearly at a loss. "Right," he said.

"Back then it was a lot less common than it is now, especially in their circles. And this was after I'd refused to marry the boy they adored back in Greenwich, the revered Howard Schmidt. Even now I hear it—'If only you'd stayed with Howard,' 'What did you ever have against Howard?'" She paused. "He was the world's biggest asshole, that's what, but try explaining that to *them."*

He waited a long moment. "I haven't even asked you yet about Professor Grabler."

"Fine," she said without notable enthusiasm. "Shoot."

"In case you can't already tell, she's one of my heroes, ever since I read her when I took night courses at Westchester Community College. *Una santa laica*."

"A secular saint?" she said. "I think that might be going a wee bit too far, don't you?"

"Si," he insisted, probing her seeming ambivalence. *"Un luchador de la gente común."*

"Okay, fine," she allowed with a smile, grasping the general meaning—a fighter for ordinary people—"if you say so. Like I say, I haven't seen her in a long time, and I really don't follow her work."

"I'm surprised, given your background together."

"Well, you know, things get in the way. Life... of course, I did see in the papers what happened up at Chester College. Very sad."

He nodded. "That's why I want to do this now. It seems so timely."

"Right, I can see that. So...." She slapped her knees and made like she was about to stand, ending their conversation.

"You haven't told me yet how you two met."

"You are persistent, aren't you?" She smiled. "It was in Madison, Wisconsin."

"Great town."

"Great place to be young, anyway. I'd dropped out of the university a couple of years before, was just knocking around, and the girl with whom I was living and I advertised for a third roommate. Francine answered it; she was just up from Texas."

"Was she calling herself Grabler then, or still Johnson?"

"Neither. Conley—she'd been married down in Texas and had just split up with the guy. Hated his guts."

Danny nodded, pleased: he'd been on target, in those intervening years there *was* another name.

"Anyway, it was a good fit—pretty soon we were raising havoc."

"How do you mean?"

Her smile seemed completely genuine. "Let's just say we were young, so we did some pretty dumb things." She paused. "Which should definitely not appear in print."

He waited a moment for her to elaborate. "You can't just leave me hanging," he said, playfully.

"Oh, you know, things I'd really rather not to get into. This was Madison in the '70s."

"Pot?"

"C'mon, everyone did pot—I think even my mother would understand that. Let's just say that looking back, some of it is pretty humiliating—and that's putting it mildly. Anyway, at some point our original roommate left, and we picked up a new one, Laure. Interesting girl. She was totally outta her head. Fit right in."

"Laura?"

"*Laure.* She was French. She was with us a couple of years, 'til she hooked up with some Hell's Angels guy—Ed. She left us and moved in with him."

Danny paused, nodding, letting this sink in, wondering what all those intensely sensitive Francine Grabler groupies would make of it all. "So how'd you guys make ends meet? Were you working?"

"Odd jobs—waitressing, whatever. I mean, we were all college dropouts. But, you know, like a lot of other people in Madison, we also got pretty involved with the shall-we-say *currents* of the time. The anti-war movement. Feminism. The self-help movement. It was pretty intense."

"So that's how you guys eventually ended up writing *I Am My Own Father, Mother and Best Friend.*

She nodded. "Really just for ourselves. I mean, neither of us was a professional writer. We couldn't believe someone actually wanted to publish it."

"Outta Sight Books."

"Outta Sight Books," she repeated.

"How come you didn't use your real names?"

She hesitated, thought a moment. "Well, you know, that made it easier," she said vaguely. "Like, all right, maybe we'd been busted a couple of times."

"Really?"

"Like I say, it was the times. And Francine thought it might hurt us with publishers. People like that—people we thought of as *straight*—were a lot less forgiving back then."

"So they never knew—"

"And what they never knew never hurt them. Or us."

"So after the success of the book—"

"It wasn't *that* successful. It's really only because of Francine that it's even still in print. But, anyway, like I say, that was the end of my literary career, and the start of hers. When Gregory came into my life, I came back east with him, and she went off and set the world on fire. I really haven't given her much thought since."

A quarter-hour later, standing by her front door, he said, "So, that wasn't too painful, was it?"

"It was fine," she replied, "long as you keep your word."

But as he walked off, there was a question he couldn't shake. *Why, for all her professed disinterest in Grabler, did she have every one of her books in her shelves?*

* * * * *

"Really sorry, Will, got nothing new," said Captain Lucas Beeban as Will walked through the door of Chester Police Department.

What's amazing is that, from the chief's tone and regretful look, it would almost have been possible to believe he *was* sorry. But this was not Will's first visit to inquire on the progress of the investigation of the attack on Grabler's residence, or the second, or the third. Indeed, by now he'd come to have a grudging admiration for the ostentatiously concerned and always good natured Chief Beeban. For his was a brand of accomplished stonewalling usually attempted only by the most practiced bureaucrats in our most corrupt big cities. It was akin to a soothing massage, designed to leave even his most demanding customers feeling better than when they walked in.

"Expected nothing else, Lucas," Will replied amiably. "Mind if I start calling you Chief Wiggum?" The reference was to the do-nothing, donut-inhaling head cop on *The Simpsons*.

"Don't know who that is, but feel free." He gave the grim but reassuring half-smile more reminiscent of Detective Joe Friday on *Dragnet*. "And don't worry, Son, we *will* get to the bottom of this."

Of course, Will also recognized that Beeban had a minefield to navigate. Officially, the investigation was a joint effort of the Chester PD and campus security, with whatever additional on-site forensics they deemed necessary provided by the state police. But the chief knew better than almost anyone else how things worked around here, which is to say, he had to constantly worry about local pols and, even more so, Chester College's president and board of trustees.

And for them, for all practical purposes, if not precisely resolved, the episode was closed. For while the identity of the person or persons who actually wielded the spray cans had not been determined, there was little doubt as to who, in the deepest recesses of their hearts, might've sympathized with the sentiments scrawled on the wall, and that was plenty good enough. In very short order punishment sufficiently severe to satisfy even Francine Grabler and her most militant supporters would be officially meted out, and that had pretty much put the issue to rest. Already, the campus was getting back to normal.

"Well, you be sure to let me know when that surveillance tape turns up." Will waved in parting. "You might try President Frank's desk drawer."

Beeban laughed and waved back. "We'll be sure to do that."

* * *

Will had been in a sour mood since the disastrous meeting in Frank's office, and things weren't looking up. But as he pulled up to Bennett's house, he made a determined effort to be upbeat. If nothing else, he knew he owed his brother a show of confidence—hell, *élan*—that he didn't feel.

"That Beeban, what a fucking asshole!" he said in greeting, his plan immediately swirling down the toilet.

"Nothing, huh?"

"They've got that damn surveillance tape somewhere!" He paused. "I hear that before he came to Chester, he was doing undercover drug work, busting kids at Albany State. That wouldn't go over with the kids here. I'm thinking my next step is to blackmail the guy."

Hey, he had to give Bennett some hope.

But his brother had a plan of his own. "You know how we've been talking about holding that press conference?"

"It's premature, Bro. Danny's getting us some good stuff, but we've got to nail it down. Otherwise those jackals will rip us to shreds."

"How about a simple one-on-one/ Just me, making the case. Not only that we had nothing to do with the attack, but raising the whole issue of academic integrity."

"Right, and who's the reporter who'll give you that fair shot? You know how it works, Bro: they'll listen sympathetically, the way they do, all misty eyed, then they'll edit the tape to make you look like Charlie Manson!"

"Actually, I've got someone in mind." He hesitated. "I've been having a couple of conversations with Becky Baker...."

"Becky Baker?" Will exploded.

"You know, off the record. That's the term, isn't it?"

Will took a deep breath to gather himself. "Look, Bennett, I know Becky Baker is attractive, and you have a thing for her."

"She's more than that! She's smart and—"

"We're talking the same Becky Baker?"

"And kind and fair, and she understands our position."

Will nodded. "And she'll roast your new-grown balls, grind 'em up and sprinkle 'em on your breakfast cereal if it'll advance her career one millimeter."

Bennett looked hurt, but not defeated. "You keep saying I should meet someone!"

Will took a moment. *How best to put this?* "Listen, Bennett, you're doing great, and I'm really proud of you. But when it comes to women—" He stopped again. "For your own good, I'll vet the next one before you let her into your life."

"Becky's very fond of me, she says I make her laugh."

He sighed. "Okay, listen, I'm your brother, I *know* you have a personality. But trust me on this, it isn't easy to find."

"Shut up, Will!" he said, glaring.

"Hey, I'm just talking strategy here, for you and for the case."

But this was spiraling way out of control, and he was grateful to be interrupted by a sharp knock at the door.

"Expecting someone?" asked Will.

"You get it. They might want someone with a personality."

Will opened the door to find Barbara Ann Doyle. "Hey," he said, surprised.

"I don't mean to barge in, but—"

"You!" shouted Bennett, appearing over Will's shoulder. "You've got a fucking nerve showing up here!"

Barbara Ann caught Will's attention and gave him an approving look; she'd heard Bennett had changed, but it was still impressive to behold in the flesh. "Listen," she said, addressing Bennett. "I understand. I do. But this couldn't wait!"

"Then take it outside, Cunt. I don't want you stinking up the place!"

"Wow!" she exclaimed, when Will followed her out to the front lawn.

"Pretty good, right? So what's this big news?"

"I have an eyewitness. Two, in fact."

"You're kidding me. Who?"

She shook her head. "Can't tell you yet."

"Will they talk?"

"I think so. I'm working on it."

"So?" He didn't need to finish the question.

"It was Grabler. She did it herself!"

* * * * *

Francine Grabler's first teaching job was at tiny Kellogg College in rural Iowa, where she was hired as an adjunct on the basis of her first book. Flipping through the school's 1981 catalogue, Danny saw she had taught a course entitled *Self Love is the Best Love*. It was evidently extremely popular with students. "Ms. Grabler is awesome," wrote one young woman on the college forum dedicated to course evaluations, subsequently archived on line. "This course changed my life!"

"Highly recommended!" wrote another. "I'm *definitely* taking her course on masturbation technique next semester!"

It was while she was at Kellogg that Grabler published her second book, *A Syllabus For Kindness*, this time in collaboration with Catherine Hyatt-Sasaki, an associate professor of Sociology at the school. But probing further, Danny ran across something entirely unexpected: following the book's publication, Grabler and her co-author had what looked to have been a bitter falling out. According to the brief accounts in the local press, Hyatt-Sasaki took her colleague to court, demanding a larger share of the book's proceeds.

Within days, Danny was standing in the cavernous lobby of the Hotel Cadillac in downtown Detroit, trying to look casual as he scanned the name tags of attendees at the annual conference of the Michigan Practitioners of Ethical and Social Well Being. Currently teaching at Alexander College in the state's Upper Peninsula, Hyatt-Sasaki was slated to appear on a panel tomorrow, but just now she was among the several hundred streaming out of the main ballroom following a presentation entitled "Undocumented Workers and S&M: Perversion or Pathway to the American Mainstream?"

Danny studied the passing faces, almost all of them grim, looking for what he presumed would be one with Japanese features. That's why he almost missed her. Tall and rail thin, she looked like an older, bespectacled version of Olive Oyl.

"Ms. Hyatt-Sasaki?"

She stopped and turned to him, squinting. "Yes?"

"I'm Jeffrey Rivera, I'm writing a piece for *The Nation*. I'm wondering if you might have a few minutes."

"*The Nation*?" she said, impressed.

"Yes."

"*The Nation magazine* is covering this conference?" For her, the fringe left-wing magazine seemed to carry the prestige of *The New York Times*, the *Washington Post* and CBS News rolled into one.

"Well," he said, sticking with the familiar, comforting story, "I'm actually just freelance, but that's where I'm hoping to place it."

She checked her watch. "Well, sure... okay."

"I'm interested in your panel," he said, as they entered the coffee shop off the lobby. "*The Father as Destroyer*. So is it your position that fathers are completely unnecessary?"

"No, no," she said, shaking her head. "As a professional, I would never speak so categorically. It is more accurate to observe that *most* fathers are destructive, and in that the vast *majority* of cases, children will be better off living with their loving single moms."

As they slid into a booth, she didn't miss a beat. "I'm most interested, as you may know, in the issue of nurturing—that is my life's work. Men can become nurturers—all humans are born with that instinct—but of course, so-called advanced Western cultures strip them of it at a young age and turn them into what I like to term *primordial beasts*."

"Primordial?"

"Because in their capacity for nurturing—for kindness generally—they differ little from primitive, single-cell organisms."

"I see."

"That said, I categorically reject the charge that I am in any way anti-male. I simply accept the truths of social science." She paused. "Shouldn't you be getting this down?"

He nodded, and pulled out a notebook.

"Is this what your article is about, the father/motherhood question?"

Before he could answer, a waitress appeared and they ordered coffees.

When the waitress left, he asked, "I'm wondering if you might fill me in a bit about yourself," leaving her question unanswered.

"It's all there in my CV. That will save you time; they have copies in the reception area."

"Yes, I've already got one." He hesitated. "Speaking of which, I wonder if I might ask you something?"

She squinted at him quizzically as the waitress poured the coffees. "Yes?"

"I couldn't help but notice you didn't include *A Syllabus for Kindness* on the CV."

Her face hardened. "No, that's right, I didn't."

"May I ask why? It's such a wonderful book."

"I see," she said, her anger rising. "So is that what this is really about, my so-called co-author?"

So-called? "Well, it just struck me," he said evenly. "It seems curious."

"I'm sorry, I've got nothing to say about that."

"And, yes, of course, Francine Grabler is always of interest, especially with what's been happening at Chester College."

She started sliding from the booth. "This interview is over, Mr.—"

"I should tell you, I've already talked to Melissa Leary."

She stopped, looked back at him. "*Melissa Leary* cooperated with you?"

He nodded. "On deep background. On the condition I not use her name."

She thought that over a moment, intrigued. "I'd ask you what she said—"

"But that would violate our agreement, and I won't do that." He paused. "I'm willing to make the same deal with you."

She slid back to where she'd been before. "I'm afraid I can't, according to the terms of our settlement."

Still, it was clear that she too, had plenty to say and she was willing, even eager, to say it.

"Right... I understand," he said. "That whole lawsuit thing must have been a real ordeal."

"You have no idea. You're not supposed to sue a colleague. I only did it because my husband at the time insisted. Because the whole thing was so unfair."

"Without going into specifics, unfair how?"

She hesitated, then shook her head. "I'm sorry."

"Anyway, were you satisfied with the settlement?"

"Satisfied? No." She gave a sudden, bitter laugh at what seemed to be some odd private joke. "It was half a loaf, but I accepted it at the time, because some people I cared about learned the truth." She paused. "But let's face it, no one remembers that now. In the end, it's just another Francine Grabler book, isn't it? And it's done a lot more for her than it ever has for me."

There was no question about that. With her gift for self-promotion, Grabler had used her writing to propel her to the highest levels of her field. She was a superstar, widely esteemed and with a permanent sinecure at one of the nation's top academic institutions. And here was Catherine Hyatt-Sasaki, stuck at a school no one's ever heard of in the wilds of northern Michigan.

"It was just *so* unfair, *so* outrageous," she repeated, shaking her head. "See, I shouldn't have let you get me started."

"So you're suggesting she really didn't contribute much," he said, pushing it.

She held up her hand. "Sorry, can't go there. I've said too much already." She paused. "You spoke to Melissa Leary... didn't she have anything to say about why she wouldn't collaborate with her on a second book?"

* * *

Several days later, still on the road, Danny was forwarded an envelope, post-marked Marquette, Michigan, that had shown up at his Bronx office. Inside was a single sheet of paper with a post-it note attached, reading simply *FYI.*

Written in a cramped, barely legible hand, it was headed *Preposal* and started with an explanatory note: *The following ideas unequivocally enclosed in this preposal for a book about kindness was prepared by myself and Ms. Hyatt-Sasaki.*

It was followed by a short paragraph:

> A wise person will say kindness is not something that you can hold or smell and such a saying is unequivocally true, but still it ruffles the waters and hurts the insides of the interior of each individual to de-privatize male power and privilege and unequivocally bring about a kinder world which is so important and is one of the main ideas among some others aimed at the readers of such a book.

* * * * *

What's amazing, mused Than, was that his friend Sergei Dubrov spoke English as well as he did. True enough, he had his accent, and his funny way of dropping definite articles and messing up his tenses. But with it all, he managed just fine. His command of the language was certainly no impediment academically, at least when it came to those subjects he cared about. In fact, in Professor Kane's highly demanding classes, Sergei's grades were rivaled only by his own.

And yet, he now realized, gazing about the Dubrov living room, he'd done it all on his own. As far as he could tell, none of the other members of the family, the people with whom he'd grown up—his parents, uncle or elderly grandmother—spoke more than a few halting words.

Not that anyone was saying much of anything at the moment. The room, with its old-fashioned drapes and heavy oak furniture was dark, but the mood was far, far darker. These people were not just disappointed, they were shell-shocked. How could it happen? It made no sense. How, after all his hard work and all their sacrifices on his behalf, had Sergei *let* it happen? To have a demanding professor, or even one that doesn't like you so awards you a B rather than an A—that is one thing, and terrible enough! But to be suspended and, even worse, facing expulsion for bad behavior!

From his armchair in the corner, Khan tried to make himself inconspicuous. He didn't belong here, with this strange, anguished family in their tiny Brighton Beach apartment, why had he ever let his friend talk him into coming? Even the smell of the place was completely alien, some bizarre, musty Old World mix of—what?—boiling meat, schnapps and body odor. Fortunately, scarcely a word had been addressed to him since their arrival, and that didn't seem likely to change. Still, occasionally one of the others would shoot a hard look his way, and he had a pretty good idea it was understood he was Sergei's confederate in this awful business, and that he was thought to bear at least some of the blame.

"Что с тобой, в.в.Путин?" his father suddenly shouted, his beefy face going red.

In a chair a few feet away, face buried in his hands, Sergei just shook his head.

"Как это случилось!"

Though the words were incomprehensible, it's not like Khan didn't understand. He'd soon have to call his parents out in Orange County with the news, and they would also be uncomprehending. Only they would be not so much angry, as profoundly, inconsolably sad. They too, had sacrificed on behalf of their children. His sister, in med school at Berkeley, would never put them through anything like this; nor would his older brother, already working at a lab in L.A.

"Позвольте мне объяснить!" offered Sergei, and his friend understood he was trying to explain.

"Хороший. Объясните!" his father said dismissively, making it clear that no explanation could possibly pass muster.

As Sergei went into his story, one familiar sound leapt out from the jumble: "Kane."

At its third mention, Mr. Dubrov held up a hand. "Кто это Kane?" he demanded. "Что вы обязаны ему?"

The sense of it could hardly be clearer: *Who is this Kane? What do you owe him?*

Sergei's words were now more rushed, as he spoke with mounting passion, and there came another familiar name: *Professor Grabler.*

Khan couldn't help note that the others listened with mounting interest and, it seemed to him, some measure of sympathy. The uncle in particular was more engaged, nodding in agreement and several times interrupting to ask for elaboration.

It was five minutes before Sergei looked his way and caught Kahn's inquiring look. "I tell whole thing, about what they do there," he said, confident. "I think they start to understand."

"We come to America for freedom," his Uncle Viktor suddenly said angrily. "This like Russia! This why we *leave* Russia!"

Khan looked at him in surprise and nodded. "It's why my grandparents left Vietnam," he said, knowing this is exactly what he would tell his parents.

But now the others went back to Russian, going back and forth, with the women also joining in. Again, over and over, there were the names, Kane and Frank, but most prominently, Grabler. The uncle was clearly the strongest personality in the family, and he spoke not only most often, but with the greatest heat. Sergei, meanwhile, seemed to be trying mainly to calm him down, but not with much success.

Abruptly, Uncle Viktor rose to his feet and nodded curtly at Khan. "Good to make your acquaintance," he said, and strode out the door.

In the long moment of silence that followed, Khan moved closer to his friend. "What was that about?" he said softly.

"He is very angry, my uncle."

"I can see that."

Sergei closed his eyes and shook his head. "I tell him 'No, Uncle, calm yourself, we are not children, we handle it ourself.'"

* * * * *

"Before we begin, the ground rules," Will announced, standing atop the Seventh Heaven bar, surveying the media arrayed before him at the tables below. "As you know, and seem to be enjoying, drinks at this establishment are on the house, courtesy of our hostess, Ms. Barbara Ann Doyle."

"Here, here," called one of the reporters, and some of the rest applauded.

Will smiled, and in acknowledgement toasted them with his own beer before continuing. "This privilege will be extended for the duration of your stay in town." He paused. "*Unless*, that is, it comes to light that you have set foot in the establishment known as Rick's Place, located on South Third Street, or have in any manner or fashion communicated with its proprietor, Richard Lampiere. Further, it should be understood that neither I nor my clients nor any member of my staff will agree to be interviewed or otherwise communicate with any media who patronize Rick's Place or in any way deal with Mr. Lampiere."

"What do you have against this guy, Will?" shouted a member of the fourth estate.

Will nodded. "I will be pleased to entertain questions on that subject on a one-on-one basis," he said. "For now, suffice it to say that it is a matter that should be of interest to your readers, viewers and listeners, one that touches on areas as varied as my own background, the corruption inherent in small town politics and the ever-fascinating world of extreme sports."

There was, to be sure, some risk involved in such an approach. Kane, for one, had argued that opening a campaign intended to establish the innocence of Wills' clients with an unprovoked attack on the lawyer's own despised former boss stood to render them all vaguely ridiculous. Will understood that, of course. But he also understood, in a way a mere academic never could, how reporters work. Unimaginative and incurious by nature, habitually given to group-think, on every issue before them they strive above all for consensus; and once it has been established, will cling to it for professional safety as they would cling to flotsam in a roiling sea. And Will's problem here was that consensus was firmly established: Francine Grabler represented goodness and virtue, her adversaries—and likely tormentors—the opposite, which is to say, in the reporters' view nothing more need be written or reported on the subject.

This reality was all too evident in the composition of the group before him. Although he'd taken pains to have releases sent to every major media outlet in the Northeast, including the major networks and news services, and follow-up calls had been made to those that had given special prominence to the attack on Grabler's residence, only fifteen reporters had shown up, most from local or small regional outlets. The only broadcast reporter, excepting Becky Baker, who hadn't bothered to bring along a crew, was a teenage kid representing a radio station in Saratoga Springs.

If making himself the center of attention was what it took to rekindle interest in the case—the *colorful* dwarf lawyer still yearning for his youthful exploits in the tossing pit—so be it. Besides, he'd been waiting nearly twenty years to stick it to that bastard Lampiere.

Already he had reason to hope the strategy was paying off. If nothing else, he had their interest.

"Now then," he said, as he began strolling the length of the bar, "to the business at hand." He paused, catching the attention of the elderly woman from *The Chester Weekly Independent*. "I am here today to issue a challenge to Professor Francine Grabler."

He stopped again to gauge their reaction, and in an instant knew he was already losing them. Scanning one face after another, he saw only blank looks or unbelieving stares.

"Please bear with me, ladies and gentlemen because questions—*vital* questions—have come to light in recent days. Questions that go to the very heart of Ms. Grabler's credibility." He extended a hand to his right. "If you please?"

In an instant, Doyle appeared and hoisted an easel onto the bar, its face page black. "What we have here," he said, grandly turning over the page to reveal the one beneath, "is an enlargement of Professor Grabler's *curriculum vitae*.

"Pointer, please?"

Doyle slapped one into his outstretched hand. "You will note the colleges where she has taught." He began smacking each in turn. "Kellogg College... Kansas Western... and then right on to Chester College. A rather spectacular rise. Most impressive."

He then pointed to the top of the page, listing her educational background. "University of Texas, both undergraduate and graduate degrees. Excellent school, as you are doubtless aware. Again, impressive!" He paused.

"But here's the thing. According to our independent investigation, she never attended U of T. Not for a single day."

The reporters exchanged shocked looks. This was astonishing information, and if true—

"Wait, hold on," called the guy who'd led the applause for the free drinks, representing the *Albany Free Press*. "What does this have to do with the attack on her home?"

There was a pause, and then someone else spoke up. "That's right, what does one thing have to do with the other?"

"Isn't this just blaming the victim?" demanded another reporter.

"Because she's a woman!"

To stem the rising tide, Will said, "You should know that we've gone to considerable lengths to have Professor Grabler here today to respond to this allegation directly. She has not responded to my calls or emails, and I can only conclude she is trying to avoid these questions." He paused, then nodded at a reporter, waving his arm like an anxious second grader. "Yes?"

The reporter pointed at the easel. "That is her *official* CV, issued by Chester College?"

"Yes, it is."

"Official... that means *real*."

This observation set multiple heads bobbing in agreement.

"If the college says it's real, it must be real!" someone shouted.

"Are you really saying *Francine Grabler* is *not* a victim? She's the most honored victim in America!"

Will held up both hands, smiling indulgently. Where the media was concerned, he was under no illusions; protecting their own is always a big part of the job. Still, this was proving even worse than he'd anticipated.

"I've had enough! This is disgusting!" one woman suddenly declared. She rose and started for the exit, and two other women immediately rose to follow.

"Sit down, bitches! He's not done!"

Barbara Ann Doyle, arms folded, was standing at the door, blocking their way.

From atop the bar, Will nodded his thanks. "I won't keep you long," he said, as the reporters sheepishly returned to their seats. "Just one other thing that might be of interest." He turned, and called, "Arthur! Arthur 3-X Perkins!"

The door to the adjacent storage room swung open, revealing a grim-faced Arthur, dressed for the occasion in dark suit, starched white shirt and bow tie. He was followed into the room by two figures clad in burkas who seated themselves on barstools immediately beneath Will.

The reporters watched awestruck, a few murmuring aloud what all were thinking: *Real live Black Muslims, right here in Chester!*

"No," corrected Will. "These two are just dressed this way to protect their identities. They are eyewitnesses to the attack on Francine Grabler's residence."

As expected, that seized the crowd's attention, and Will let the tension build a long moment. Then he glanced down. "Can you tell us what you saw that night?"

There was a pregnant pause before the one on the right spoke. "We were walking on South Elm, near her house...." she began, in a husky whisper intended to disguise her voice.

"Whose house?" Will gently prodded.

"Professor Grabler's."

"And how far away would you say you were?"

"Maybe fifty yards. Not very far."

"And what did you see?"

"Professor Grabler. She seemed to be writing something on the wall."

"Could you see what she was writing?"

"It was too dark."

"But you're certain it was her?"

"Yes."

"And you...." He tapped the other on the shoulder with his foot. "You saw this also?"

The other nodded, as per the deal. It was hard enough getting her to show up at all. Speaking was out of the question.

"And you corroborate this? That it was definitely Francine Grabler writing on her own wall?"

She hesitated a moment, but nodded again.

"Thank you for your courage and your commitment to the rule of law."

With that, their ordeal complete, Arthur helped them from the stools and led them back to the storage room.

Will turned back to the press, not knowing what to expect.

"Why were they wearing those things?" demanded someone.

"I believe I explained that," he said. "Next... you?"

"An anonymous accusation! This is about the worst victim blaming ever!"

"Is that a question?" he asked. "Because you should know they are prepared to give sworn statements to the proper authorities and, if necessary, to testify under oath."

"That was some cheap stunt!"

"It was totally biased against Professor Grabler. She could sue for libel!"

On some level, Will couldn't help almost enjoying the spectacle. It was truly a wonder to behold, this pack of hacks deluding themselves before his eyes that they were zealots for individual liberty.

Smiling, he gave up. "Okay, show's over. Feel free to have another drink."

"Or three!" called one of the reporters, drawing laughter from the others. "Any chance we can also get some free eats?"

Will turned to Doyle, who rolled her eyes, but nodded. "Just appetizers... the left side of the menu only."

"My favorite side!" someone laughed, the earlier unpleasantness forgotten.

* * * * *

"We're here to serve the community, Sir," said the attractive young police woman, and indeed, her little nameplate identified her as *SGT. KAREN WOJTINSKI, Community Service Officer*.

"So you're saying I can have full access to the records?" asked Danny. "Because what I'm after might take some time. It could be a lengthy search."

He wasn't about to admit that while he more or less knew what he hoped to find, there was considerable question whether it was there at all.

"We'll help you in any way we can, Sir. It's not only our responsibility, it's the law, under both local ordinance and Wisconsin's Open Records statute."

Danny nodded, delighted. Hard to believe that a mere half-hour earlier, walking down University Avenue adjacent to the campus a mile away, he had been thinking how much he hated Madison, with its relentlessly PC bookshops and overpriced coffee bars, its vegan restaurants and redundant bike shops—but nary a hardware store or fast food joint in sight. One of those college towns that not only forgot to grow up, it basked in smug, post-revolutionary contempt for anyone that did.

Yet, amazingly, it was working for him. For in Madison, more than anywhere else in America, the lunatics truly had taken over the asylum. And one result was that the local police, after decades of having been denounced as pigs and sadists, investigated for brutality and malfeasance and editorialized against by the media, had been reformed into neutered lapdogs by local pols ideologically indistinguishable from those in the Politburo in the Soviet heyday. Danny could scarcely believe it. The cops here were more like social workers or, in the case of pretty Sgt. Wojtinski, helpful librarians.

He asked for clarification. "So it'll all be here... every arrest, even for misdemeanors, shoplifting, things like that?"

"Absolutely," she nodded. "But I do have to ask—are you requesting this information because you're a business owner?"

He was surprised by the question. "Uh...no, I'm not."

"Because," she added with a sudden note of severity, "I am obliged by law to inform you that discrimination against employees or potential employees on the basis of a criminal record is forbidden in the state of Wisconsin."

"Well, no, that wouldn't apply to me. I'm really just searching for... my own purposes."

"Fine," she said, the sunshine returning. "Let me show you to the research area."

She motioned him through a door and into a carpeted room with a dozen or so tables, each bearing a computer, several already occupied.

He took a seat and she pointed at the screen. "Just input the person's name," she said in a whisper, as if this actually were a library, "including the middle name if you have it. Add any additional information you might have, such as birth date and address. That will naturally make the search more efficient."

"Got it, Officer, thank you."

"If you need further assistance, don't hesitate to ask."

He opened his notebook to the appropriate page and typed in the first name: MAYHEW, MARTHA.

No matches found, came the instantaneous response.

He typed in: MAYHEW, MELISSA

No matches found.

LEARY, MELISSA

No matches found.

Checking his notes, Danny spotted the name of her spurned suitor.

SCHMIDT, MELISSA

In a millisecond, seven entries appeared.

The list ran by date, starting with the most recent, and his heart fell when he noted it was 7/28/09, for *Battery against husband.*

The next two arrests, dated 2008 and 2006, were on the same charge. Obviously a different Melissa Schmidt, and not one he'd ever be interested in meeting.

But then there was a jump of more than twenty-five years, back to the early 1980s.

Jackpot!

This Melissa Schmidt—Melissa M. Schmidt, presumably for Mayhew—was first nailed on May 4,

1981 on a misdemeanor charge of petty theft—shoplifting—the complainant being Anthony Vucco, Assistant Manager of Deitz Foods on State Street. There was no indication of what might have been taken, only that its approximate value was $35. While no disposition of the case was given, Danny figured the charge had either been dismissed or disposed of with a modest fine.

Melissa M. Schmidt's second arrest, in November, 1982, occurred in the parking lot of a Howard Johnson's Motor Inn and was recorded as *aggravated petty theft and malicious mischief against a motor vehicle.* The target was not the car itself, a blue, 1979 Ford Granada two-door sedan, but its *out-of-state (Indiana) license plate.*

Danny made a note, his pulse starting to pick up. *What the hell is this about?*

The next arrest was less than four months later, in March, 1983. This one was for Third Degree assault, another misdemeanor. The complaint—later dropped—asserted that *Miss Schmidt attacked Allen Renzo, an employee of Wilson Ag, a supplier of agricultural products in Evansville, with her fists and fingernails after being informed she would be unable to buy the product she desired, as her credit card was no good.*

Recreating the scene, Danny guessed that Melissa might well have walked into the place high, and also that her rocky relationship with her parents might have had something to do with her loss of credit. Though he of course couldn't know for certain what she'd been trying to buy, by now he had at least a faint suspicion about that also.

Her last listed arrest added considerable weight to that suspicion. This time the charge was far more serious: aggravated breaking and entering, a felony. She was discovered and held by a night watchman attempting to enter a storage shack owned by Quinn and Powers Construction at a site on the outskirts of Milwaukee where a factory complex was under construction.

This time she did two weeks before being bailed out—presumably by her parents. There was no record of the case having come to trial.

Danny sat back and took a deep breath. To his experienced eye, a definite pattern was developing. Still, that's all it was so far, a pattern. More to the point, Melissa was ultimately not his concern. Now he typed in the name GRABLER, FRANCINE.

No matches found. Not that he'd expected any.

JOHNSON, FRANCINE

No matches found.

CONLEY, FRANCINE

No matches found.

"Shit," he muttered, having figured that was his best shot, the name she'd brought up here from her Texas marriage.

He waited a moment longer, then got to his feet. He started to his left, toward the community service lounge, then veered right instead, in the direction of the men's room. His hair was his best feature, and a twenty-second comb couldn't hurt.

"Hi, again."

Sergeant Wojtinski looked up from her computer screen and gave him her official smile. "How may I help you, Sir?"

"I'm just wondering. Is it ever possible to locate a person's records from just a first name?"

"Only a first name?" She shook her head. "I'm afraid it would be too common."

"This one's not, it's very unusual. Laure."

"Laura?"

He smiled. "I made the same mistake. Laure. L-A-U-R-E. It's French."

"Laure—you're right, that's a new one on me. We don't have any of those where I come from."

"Oh, yes, where's that?"

She blushed slightly; this was uncomfortably close to flirting. "I'm sure you never heard of it. Hurley. A little town up north."

"Anyway, I tried it on the other machine, and an 'insufficient information' thing came up. I was thinking there might be a more advanced program or something." He paused. "You know, as a law enforcement tool."

She looked at him evenly, seeming to think it over, but not contradicting him.

"I realize it's not routine, but if it's not too much trouble."

"Hold on," she said with a decisive nod. She rapidly typed in a code, followed by LAURE. "Any idea of likely dates? To narrow it down?"

"It would probably be the early '80s."

She typed that in and waited half a beat. Then, "Laure Ferran" and she spelled the last name. "Does that sound right?"

"I think so, yes!"

She leaned in a bit closer to read. "Oh, wow! Quite a girl!"

"What do you mean?"

"First entry, 10/22/81, for solicitation."

"You're kidding me!"

Unbidden, he moved behind the counter and peered over her shoulder.

"There's just one other entry," she said, "dated 5/18/83, breaking and entering."

But Danny was already reading it himself. It was at the site of the Quinn and Powers Construction project, and this more complete record listed all those arrested at the scene: FERRAN, LAURE; SCHMIDT, MELISSA M.; and a third suspect, JOHNSON, CONLEY F.

* * * * *

Francine Grabler had considered canceling the interview, but in the end thought better of it. She was nothing if not professional. Unlike so many authors, she had always embraced the promotional side of the job, letting company publicists know right up front that she was willing to do any and all media, no matter how podunk the market. It was a personal point of pride that no one else out there had her amazing ability to say the same things for months on end and still sound fresh. Even for a writer of her stature with a built-in audience, books don't sell themselves.

Besides which, today's interview, with NPR's Deborah Klein, was the kind she especially relished, featuring as it surely would fat softballs lobbed by a longtime friend and ally. And though she was into the second month of her promotional slog for *The Romance of Self-Adoration*, many of the network's snob listeners had surely missed her appearances on the morning shows or even *The View*.

Still, as the hour drew near, there was no familiar rush of adrenaline. Retreating to her bedroom, she lay down and closed her eyes, her mind racing. There was no need to really worry, of course. She'd had tough moments before, plenty of them—her enemies were as relentless as they were vicious—so, yes, they were out there again with their charges and slurs—*anonymous*, of course. Once again she would stand up to them, and reveal them as the monsters they were. Wasn't it this, after all—her willingness to not just proclaim truth to power, but to throw herself into the very gears of the patriarchal machine—that made her the beloved figure she was?

Abruptly, the phone on the table by the bed sounded and, glancing at the clock, she was surprised to see it was already 3:55. She reached for it, but hesitated, her hand suspended. She stayed that way for all five rings, until the phone went silent. Seconds later, her mobile sounded; then, a moment after that, her text message; then the land line again.

There was silence for a minute or so; then, just as she was rising from the bed, it rang again—probably her publicist this time, or her agent.

"That's all right," she said aloud. "It's just this once; they'll reschedule." *What I need right now is me time.* She'd come to that realization yesterday, so her bag was already packed. Snatching it up, she headed for the door.

The streets bordering the campus were quiet this late Friday afternoon. Still, preoccupied as she was, she failed to notice the car down the street, pulling out to follow her.

* * * * *

When Will's eyes fluttered open, he was momentarily startled. Floating just above, as if in some hideous drug induced fantasy, were six glittery girlish fairies. It took an instant to sink in: Bloom, Flora and Disney's other ludicrously named Winx Club girls suspended from the ceiling by string, his brother's latest pathetic attempt to buy his daughter's goodwill.

"Rock bottom," he muttered, sitting up in Casey's small bed. "Rock damn bottom."

"Will, get in here!"

"What, goddammit?"

"Just get your ass in here!"

"All right, I'm coming!" he called, once again caught short by Bennett's newfound air of command.

Dashing into the living room in his pajamas, he saw that Becky Baker was on the TV. She was in the middle of a stand-up before Francine Grabler's freshly repainted home. "The much-loved Chester College professor whose home was recently the target of a terroristic hate crime," she soberly intoned. "We are told that Professor Grabler did not appear to teach a 4:00 p.m. class yesterday, and campus sources tell WFUN News that she has not been seen since late Friday afternoon when she reportedly left this residence—the same residence that three weeks ago was defaced with crude and bigoted slogans."

"She's missing?"

Bennett nodded. "Looks like it."

"That bitch! God*damn* her!"

His brother looked at him, confused.

"It's a goddamn distraction! The shit's starting to hit the fan and she's trying to change the narrative! And you know what? They'll let her get away with it!"

Bennett pretended to consider this a moment. "So what do you think of Becky's outfit? I like her in blue, don't you?"

"Will you stop it with that stupid girl? She's part of the problem!"

Bennett looked hurt. "You don't know her, Will. She wants to tell our side; they just won't let her."

"Who's *they*? You idiot, *she's* they!"

"You just don't know her," Bennett repeated defiantly. "You won't even give her a chance. *I* say she looks great in blue!"

* * *

Within twenty minutes, a half-dozen news vans had joined the one from WFUN in the visitor's parking lot beyond the administration building, and by late morning the big time network correspondents from the city were starting to arrive, immaculately coiffed and in beautifully tailored suits. Chester students, many of whom had been weeping without cease since hearing the unspeakable news, turned their way with red faces and runny noses, gazing with unembarrassed awe. The correspondents were used to this, and took it as their due, but today acknowledged it only with sober nods. Greeting one another with grim handshakes, they made their way to Grabler's home, the focus of all activity.

Already, a makeshift shrine was in place on the sidewalk before the walkway, at its center a life-sized photograph of the missing woman, in a white caftan, a beatific smile on her face and arms extended in welcome. Surrounding it, in an ever growing pile, were photographs of Grabler and heartfelt notes written by her anguished admirers, copies of her books, stuffed animals and countless floral bouquets. Too, there were masses of poison ivy, which Grabler had publicly embraced as her personal favorite plant. A hand-lettered sign accompanied one batch and quoted her: *Forever bullied, long a victim of ridicule and malice, yet in the end, do we know a stauncher defender of self?*

The correspondents joined the growing throng, staring in reverent silence, and a couple ostentatiously pulled out pens and wrote notes of their own to add to the pile.

In truth, at this juncture there was precious little to report. While the correspondents for the all-news cable stations were the ones most obviously on the job, occasionally moving off to the side to do live on-camera updates, the same phrases echoed through every such report: "No new information." "Keeping our fingers crossed." "Keeping vigil." "Hoping for the best."

At noon, as promised, President Frank and Police Chief Beeban held a joint press conference on the steps of the administration building.

"Thank you all for being here," Frank began, the pain etched on his face. "As you know, we have not heard from our beloved colleague, Distinguished Professor Francine Grabler, for over three days now... and counting." His voice cracked, but he quickly regained his composure and nodded at Beeban. "Chief."

"Like President Frank says, we are highly concerned." He paused, then, for emphasis, "To the utmost. Especially in light of previous recent events. We'll take questions."

Two dozen hands went up, and Beeban pointed at one. "Yes."

"Are you suggesting foul play?"

"I'm not suggesting anything. I'm just suggesting this is no regular case, and I think you know what I mean by that. We all know this fine woman was traumatized by what happened to her. We can only hope she's just gone off to lick her wounds, so to speak." He pointed. "Yes."

"You have no leads as to where she might have gone, or with whom?"

"We have some ideas. As President Frank was telling me earlier, she is a woman of many pieces—"

"Parts," Frank clarified softly.

"And she's her own person. She has a worldwide network of admirers and colleagues, so there's that. And everyone knows she is a lover of the great outdoors, so—"

"And a defender," Frank added meaningfully. "A great *defender* of nature. Someone who, as she once told me herself, shows wild grass the respect of treading softly and embraces even sewer rats as colleagues in life's great adventure."

This appeared to have a profound effect on the listeners, who fell into silence.

"All we can do is keep our vigil," Frank added, "and treat one another with the kindness she has so long epitomized."

"And pray," spoke up a sonorous-voiced newsman.

There was another silence, this time awkward. "No, we don't do that. We don't like to make anyone uncomfortable."

"Oh, right," said the chagrinned reporter, his gaucherie exposed before the world and, far, far worse, his colleagues. "Just an expression."

* * *

Though the Milwaukee-based Quinn and Powers Construction firm went belly up in the early '90s, the roster of its principle employees was on file in the public library on West Wisconsin Avenue. Studying the list of those who'd been in place in the early '80s, Danny jotted down a number of likely names to check out further.

The first one, Stephen Bliss, formerly the firm's deputy director of security, proved to be all he needed. He was still more or less in the area, just an hour and a half north in Appleton. Even better, he was in the investigations racket himself, with a specialty in what his LinkedIn profile described as *domestic tranquility insurance*.

Danny set up the meeting on line, without specifying what it was about. This seemed okay with Bliss, whom he guessed took him for just another cuckolded husband, and suggested they meet at an Appleton restaurant called The Melting Pot. Danny had just sat down and ordered a cup of coffee when Bliss walked in. In his mid-60's and several inches over six feet, he looked for all the world like an old time mountain man: weather-beaten face, unkempt gray beard, formidable belly beneath a faded flannel shirt. Danny's first impulse was to wonder how this guy could possibly go unnoticed skulking around suburban malls after cheating spouses.

He needn't have worried.

"I'm pretty much retired now," Bliss quickly let him know. "Gave up my office and use this place instead." He laughed, revealing a mouthful of bright white dentures. "Overhead's real low, usually just coffee."

Danny raised his cup in salute.

"So what can I do for you, young man?"

This time there was no need for bullshitting, a rare treat for Danny. He reached in his pocket and slid a card across the table—a real one, with his actual name, address and profession.

Bliss furrowed his brow and took from his shirt pocket a pair of black-rimmed eyeglasses with tape on the bridge.

"You've come a long way," he said, after studying it a moment.

"I have, yes."

"Well, you want me to guess what for?"

"Easiest job you'll ever have. I just need some information about an incident back when you were with Powers and Quinn."

Bliss studied him, noncommittal.

"Something that happened in May, 1983."

"That was a long time ago, Son. Another life...."

"At the time, the company had a project going in north Milwaukee, federally funded housing."

"Well, sure, 'course I remember that. Covington Gardens—it was a huge deal." He laughed, showing his teeth again. "Instant slum—you should see 'em today. Millions right down the toilet."

"There was an attempted break-in one night at one of your work sheds. A night watchman stopped it."

He nodded. "Sure. Those three spoiled rotten little girls."

"Exactly," Will said, relieved. "Are you saying you saw the girls first hand?"

He nodded. "At the arraignment—I was there representing our outfit, trying to see to it they got their just desserts, which of course they didn't. The three of 'em were smirking like it was all a big game."

"So what happened to them?"

"Oh, they had them in the county lockup a little while, 'til their mommies thought they'd learned a lesson, and then they bailed 'em out. Never showed up for the trial. It's not like forfeiting a few thousand in bail was anything at all to 'em."

Danny couldn't help but note how much apparent bitterness remained all these years later. "It really stuck in your craw, didn't it?"

"I just saw far too much of that crap back then." He paused. "You still see it now."

"Let me ask you," he said evenly, "what do you suppose they were after that night?"

"It wasn't a damn wheelbarrow, I can tell you that much, or a damn cement mixture. Explosives, that's what!"

Danny nodded. That confirmed what he'd been thinking. "Good thing your guy stopped them."

"That time. But we had other break-ins those years where no one got nabbed, and we weren't the only construction outfit that got hit. We didn't publicize 'em 'cause we didn't want to encourage the sons of bitches, but they happened. And we saw the results." He shook his head, adding unnecessarily, "It still burns my ass!"

"They were bad news," Danny agreed. "They did a lot of harm."

"Let's not mince words—they were *evil.* They were *terrorists*, is what! And too many of 'em got away with it!"

Danny nodded gravely. "Right."

Bliss still hadn't asked what Danny was looking to do with the information or who had sent him, and he didn't seem about to.

"Well," Danny said, reaching into his jacket pocket. "I can't thank you enough, Mr. Bliss."

He pulled two C-notes from his wallet and handed them across the table, but Bliss pulled back and held up his hands, palms out. "Forget it. Professional courtesy." He stood up and extended a huge hand. "Just go out there and get the job done."

* * *

In his car around the corner from the restaurant, Danny studied the list he'd been compiling of terrorist incidents that had occurred during the years in question in this part of the country. Formulated mainly from brief accounts in local papers, it was far longer than he'd ever have suspected, including a dozen kidnappings and jailbreaks, and more than thirty bombings, many of them never solved. The targets were government offices, banks or corporate headquarters, as well as academic research facilities deemed by the perpetrators to be part of the despised "military-industrial complex" or, in the case of animal testing facilities and logging companies, enemies of nature or the environment. Additionally, there were innumerable robberies linked to the perpetrators, the most common targets having been smaller banks and gun shops.

What most surprised him was how little attention these self-styled guerillas had received. Unlike their brethren in the Weather Underground, who publicly romanticized themselves as heirs to the great and noble revolutionary figures of the past, these shunned publicity, instead operating in tiny, highly disciplined cells, essentially on their own. This made them extremely difficult to catch, especially in a region like this, where many viewed them with frank sympathy. And even when they were caught, law enforcement tended to be undercut at every turn by progressives, including those on the bench.

Now, reviewing the list, Danny focused on a handful of unsolved bombings from late 1982 through early 1984.

But there was one in particular that riveted his interest, and he triple circled it in red: the November 1983 bombing of a medical research facility on the University of Wisconsin's Eau Claire campus. This time, not only had there been extensive property damage, but a Jamaican student, moonlighting as a janitor, was killed.

* * * * *

"You go to the press conference?" Kane asked.

The bartender was lugging around cases of beer behind the bar, so Will put his phone on speaker. "Why would I do that to myself? I'm here at Seventh Heaven. I'll be seeing the bastards soon enough."

"Okay, good. That's what I want to talk to you about."

"Listen, Alex, I'll handle them."

"I know that. But it's not about me." He hesitated. "Can you make sure my kids don't get dragged into it? They've suffered enough already."

Will looked up at Doyle beside him, and she shook her head in sympathy.

"I'll do my best, Alex. They're not around, are they?"

"'Course not, they're suspended."

"Well, that helps." He paused. "Frankly, I don't think they're uppermost on anyone's mind right now, anyway."

"They are on mine, goddammit! They're good kids, and gifted, and I put them in this fix! The least I can do is try to see they still have a future!"

"Right. Of course." He paused as the door to the place swung open. "Oh, shit, here they are. I'll get back to you."

Sure enough, predictable as the wildebeest migration of the southern Serengeti, the media came trooping through the door. As Will knew it would, word of the open bar had gone viral.

He watched as one especially weasly looking guy cut ahead of the others and snatched three beers from the bar, then retreated to a corner and began typing furiously.

His curiosity aroused, Will sidled over. "Excuse me."

The guy looked up and started. "What? I'm under deadline here!" He turned away and resumed typing.

"Just thought I'd introduce myself." He offered his hand. "Will Tripp. I represent Dr. Alexander Kane."

The other stopped and, giving him a once over, offered his hand. "It was limp and damp. "Delighted, but I'm still under deadline." He resumed his typing.

This seemed odd, since the hour was early; besides which, there was no fresh news. Then he spotted the tag on the guy's computer bag: Ellis Markham, NYT. As if he needed another reason to despise the guy.

But knowing that every other pansy-assed journalist in the room would follow his lead, he forced himself to smile. "Mind if I ask your angle?"

The guy looked up again, deeply irritated. "Read it in the paper."

"I only ask because, trust me, this story's a lot more complicated than it seems."

"Will you please? I've got work to do!"

"Fair enough," Will said, still smiling. But before turning away, he snatched up two of the beers. "Sorry, limit of one to a customer."

He waited a few minutes after Markham stopped typing before checking in on *The Times* site. Appearing on the paper's virtual front page, the story was headlined *Chester College Keeps Vigil for Missing Professor*. It began

"The Chester College community is fearing the worst today, following the disappearance of the beloved professor recently targeted for abuse by rival faculty members. While none of those faculty members has yet been formally charged in the bias attack against the home of Professor Francine Grabler, several face severe sanctions imposed by the school, and both college officials and local police are openly speculating on a possible link between the earlier incident and Ms. Grabler's disappearance."

Standing at the bar, Will snapped his phone shut and surveyed the room with disgust. *God, how I hate them! Not just the* Times *bastard, but the lowing herd sure to follow in his wake!*

Instantly, he moved into damage control mode, eyeing a corner table where a pair of network honchos, a man and a woman, were into their second drink.

"So, whaddya think?" he said, ambling over.

As always keenly aware of the effect he had on those taken unawares, Will waited for the momentary awkwardness to give way to slavishly eager-to-please behavior.

"Oh, hello!" said the woman, the rictus grin beneath her helmet hair showing her there-but-for-the-grace horror.

"Just wondering about your thoughts so far...."

They both stared, mouths slightly agape. Did he want an autograph, or just to bask a couple of moments in their presence? Then it hit him: there was something else going on here. They were both married, but not to each other; something that could prove useful.

He gave a quick, self-depreciatory laugh. "Sorry, I'm Will Tripp. I'm the attorney for Professors Kane and

Tripp, who have unfortunately, and very unfairly, gotten mentioned in connection with this terrible story."

"Oh, I see, yes." The guy extended his hand, taking for granted Will knew who he was. "Absolutely tragic," he said, apparently not recognizing the names of Will's clients. "Devastating. All any of us can do is hope for the best."

"Exactly," agreed his colleague.

"Absolutely." He paused. "I'm just wondering, how much do you know about her? Have you looked into her background?"

"The professor?" replied the guy. "Just what everyone knows. She's incredible, one of the best. Gifted."

"And there are some real crazies around here who've been out to get her," added the woman meaningfully. "Quite a story."

With a snap of his wrist, Will produced a pair of cards, and handed one to each. "Those would be my clients."

They exchanged a quick, panicked look. "Listen, we didn't mean to suggest that—"

"Hey." Will cut her off with a raised hand. "No apology necessary. I know perfectly well what people are saying. I just want to urge you, if at all possible, within the limits of your professional obligations, to keep an open mind."

"Of course," the man said, affronted. "We always do."

"Good, thanks, that's all I ask." He gave a conspiratorial wink. "Enjoy your stay. Like I say, what happens in Chester, stays in Chester... usually."

Will moved on to another table of reporters, and more or less repeated the process, humbling himself in the hope of forging a working relationship with these jackasses. If nothing else, he figured he was at least setting himself up to be the go-to guy for the *pro forma* reaction from the other side aimed at lending pretend balance to their incredibly biased stories.

The whole spectacle was so dispiriting that midway through he placed a call to Bennett. If Becky Baker got her pretty ass over to Seventh Heaven, he was prepared to give her an exclusive one-on-one. His only condition—surely never to be honored, but what the hell—was that she run the interview uncut.

When Becky showed up with her crew, he led them to a table less than ten feet away from Markham, wanting to be sure *The Times* man heard every word.

"So Mr. Tripp," began Baker, leaning earnestly forward, "just so the viewers know it's not a problem with our camera, you *are* a Little Person."

"Yes, I am, Becky, though I prefer the term *dwarf*."

"And despite your impediment you are a lawyer, here representing Professor Alexander Kane and also Professor Bennett Tripp, who is also your brother, in the Francine Grabler disappearance case."

"I am representing them, yes. Though I want to stress no charges have been filed against my clients, and I have no reason to expect there will be, since neither has anything to do with it."

"Despite what many people seem to believe—"

"I must tell you, sadly, that from the very beginning the facts of this case have been badly misrepresented, not only by the Chester College administration but in the way it has been covered. I'm hopeful that as we move ahead, the media will begin looking more closely at Professor Grabler. Because, frankly, this is someone with a great deal to hide, someone who—"

"Perhaps, but isn't the issue now her safety? And don't we also have to look at hate?"

"I personally believe this so-called disappearance is a ruse and a stunt, designed to distract people's attention from the real facts."

"Umm hmmm," she said blandly, staring down at her notes as she formulated her next question.

"Tell me, Becky, have you ever heard of Aimee Semple MacPherson?"

"Pardon me?" she said, looking up.

"She was a well-known radio evangelist in the 1920s, revered very much in the way Francine Grabler is now. But she had a terrible secret that was about to come out—she'd been having an affair with a married man—so she staged her own disappearance."

"Are you saying Ms. Grabler is having an affair?" She paused a half-beat. "And, if so, what's wrong with that?"

"I'm just saying the cases are comparable in that—"

All at once, he was aware of almost everyone in the room simultaneously reaching for his phone.

"They've found her!" shouted the first to read his text. 'Someplace up in the Adirondacks!"

"Oh my God!"

"Oh Jesus!"

Around Will all hell was breaking loose as every reporter in the place was on his feet, hurriedly gathering up his stuff.

"See that?" Will told Becky. "No problem."

"No problem?" said *The Times* guy in scornful disbelief, bolting for the door. "She's dead!"

* * * * *

The body had been discovered by a pair of hikers in a ravine near Panther Gorge, one of the most remote spots in the Adirondacks' High Peaks region. She was fully fitted out in hiking gear, her North Face Recon backpack still in place, a top-of-the-line MontBell all-weather sleeping bag inside, along with two days' supply of food, ranging from fortified seaweed to freeze-dried ice cream sandwiches. The narrow trail from which she had fallen snaked along a rock face 140 feet above.

In trying to figure out what had happened, investigators had few clues. It was a testament to her fitness that she was there at all, since the rugged terrain tended to draw only experienced hikers, most of them far younger, and the majority of those male. There were no indications of struggle, either on the body or on the trail, and no witnesses reported having encountered her on the lightly traveled path. Her car, an experimental Lexus RX 400h hybrid fitted with an auxiliary Nissan Leaf electric engine, was in the lot by the park entrance, more than six miles away. Surveillance cameras indicated more than one hundred other vehicles had entered and departed the grounds over the period in question, but the cameras were serviced by government workers under union rules, so neither their occupants nor their license plates were discernible.

Within hours of the body's discovery, the state police issued a pro forma release to the effect that they were "working diligently to unearth the cause of this terrible tragedy."

At Chester College, meanwhile, shock quickly gave way to a depth of grief unprecedented in the school's long history. Within hours, every building on campus was swathed in black crepe—the grounds superintendent had ordered miles of the stuff in anticipation of just such a gruesome outcome—and within a day hundreds of students of both sexes were wearing muu muus in Grabler's honor.

But too, there was a powerful undercurrent of rage, and no hesitation at all about what—and who—was to blame. The student paper, *The Chestonian*, rushed out a special edition, with the front page given over to a cartoon that summed it up: having reached the top of a mountain labeled *KINDNESS*, Professor Grabler was being pushed to her death by an enormous hand labeled *HATE*. The caption proclaimed, *She has been to the mountaintop!* invoking Martin Luther King.

As Will sat on a bench in the quad, studying it, one of the reporters to whom he'd been sucking up happened by.

"Pretty powerful stuff," he observed of the cartoon, admiringly.

"It's total fucking BS."

"We're reprinting it on our front page and thinking of hiring the kid who did it. Great stuff."

"Don't you guys care anything about the facts?"

The guy liked Will and knew he was a great character, so understood when his leg was being pulled. "Right, harrumph, harrumph, the *facts*," he imitated as he started off, mock huffy, smiling Will's way. "*Don't you guys care anything about the facts?*"

Already Will had given Kane and Bennett firm instructions to lay low. Though generally pretty indifferent to what others regarded as threats, he had the growing sense that there were people around here today capable of anything.

Alas, among them was the town's chief law enforcement officer.

"No chance," snapped Chief Beeban, when Will stopped by his office to ask whether measures might be taken to guarantee his clients' safety. "I'd shoot 'em myself if I could."

"Better make damn sure the surveillance cameras are out for that one," Will tried jollying him along.

But this time Beeban was having none of it. "Show a little respect, Tripp. What's wrong with you? Because you're not doing yourself or your clients any good with that attitude."

"What attitude is that, Chief?"

"That they're not responsible for the death of this wonderful woman."

"Great, fine, then go ahead and charge them! Because I have a dozen witnesses that'll say they were both in Chester the entire weekend!"

"Don't press it," said Beeban, glaring. "I just might. I have solid information that Alexander Kane is a stone cold killer, with a history of targeting those of other backgrounds and beliefs."

"And I just might hit you with a libel suit," Will shot back, guessing the likely source of the slander was Kane's ass-licking ex-lawyer, Jason Paul. "Lemme ask you something, Wiggum. You ever even consider that there are plenty of other people who despised that woman?"

Oddly, such a possibility seemed to take the chief completely by surprise.

"Like, for instance, all the angry parents who sent their kids to this place and watched her turn them into zombies," offered Will, answering the question Beeban refused to ask. This particular insight was courtesy of Marty Katz, a French Revolution buff who had more than once volunteered how good he thought Grabler's head would look on a pike. "Are you aware there are support groups for parents of Chester students? A lot of those poor people end up needing psychiatric care!" He was winging it, of course, but found himself enormously pleased by how it was sounding. "Have you even considered how much some of the *other* faculty around here hated her, including some of her supposed allies? What, you don't think there was jealousy, and anger, and bitterness when she'd cut them out for grants, or hog all the attention for stuff they did together?"

"Get out of here, Tripp! Now!"

"Sure, Chief," he said, feeling immensely better for having off loaded some of his anger on Beeban. "Of course, I'm of the school that she just did everyone a favor and offed herself, because she knew there was a lot of shit about to come out." He smiled. "But that's just me."

That was a harsher variation of the line Will was also peddling before the cameras, when asked, as he had been at least half a dozen times already, about his clients' responsibility. He was adamantly denying, proposing alternative scenarios and gently casting aspersions on Grabler's character even while pretending to admire her. While he strongly suspected it wasn't having much impact, since no reporter followed up by asking what new information, if any, he actually had, he knew he made a sympathetic figure on camera, which certainly couldn't hurt the cause and definitely helped his ego.

President Frank, for his part, was even less happy with Will's theories than Beeban.

"You're trying to pretend the issue is what happened yesterday," he said angrily when the lawyer tracked him down exiting the administration building.

"According to the law, that is *precisely* the issue. There is no evidence that either of my clients was involved in this—" He reined himself in. "*Tragedy* in any way, shape or form, and you'd damn well better stop suggesting otherwise!"

Frank shook his head adamantly, barely able to keep his composure. "No, no, no! Whether or not it happened the way you suggest is immaterial. What matters is *why* it happened. And we know the answer: hate!"

"So you admit it: she killed herself!"

"That's exactly my point! If so, I salute her for it! She died as she lived, epitomizing, *embracing* her victimhood! Obviously, she had no alternative!"

Will studied the college president a long moment, standing there in his muu muu. "Have you no sense of shame, Sir?" he said, indignant to the core, summoning up the lines that famously sank the progressives' arch-villain *número uno,* Joe McCarthy. "At long last, have you left no sense of shame?"

Frank stared back at him, eyes bulging and mouth agape. What was this? These were special lines, reserved for him and his alone!

He still hadn't formulated a response when Will's phone sounded. Checking the number, he saw it was Danny Valenzuela, out in the Midwest.

"What?"

"I need you out here right away!"

Beside him, President Frank had regained his bearing and was shooting him daggers. "Incorrect, Sir," he mumbled. "*You* have no sense of shame!"

"Are you out of your mind?" Will said. "With what's happening here!"

"Exactly! I wouldn't ask otherwise! Just be on the first plane!"

* * * * *

"Sorry," Danny said, greeting Will at the airport ramp, "but I need you to be in on this."

"I hope so 'cause those jokers are just itching to hit Kane and my brother with a murder rap, and I had to leave them in the care of my associates."

"Marjorie Spivak and what's-his-name?" Danny said, starting to laugh.

"That's right, Arthur 3-X Perkins, and it's not funny!" Then, despite himself, Will cracked up too.

In the car, Danny filled him in. "Remember Laure Ferran?"

Will had just been reviewing Danny's reports on the plane. "The French girl arrested at the construction site."

"I tracked her down—through an old wedding announcement, of all things. She never left the area."

"Here's betting it was a shotgun wedding... with a real shotgun." Will smirked.

"I'd take that bet. I was on the phone with them yesterday, and they came off as pretty traditional."

"Oh, yeah?" he said with interest.

"She even took the guy's name, goes by Reichenbach now." He paused. "Reichenbach. Know what, I should get a bonus just for keeping track of all the names."

"Okay, so?"

"It was a terrific call. Couldn't have gone better. They're really excited to meet you." He checked his watch. "Their place is out in New Berlin. Shouldn't take more than half an hour."

"They're *excited?*" Will said. "Do they know what we're after?"

"That's the point, they do. Not the specifics, of course, but I gave them a general idea." He turned to glance at Will. "It was crazy. It was like they actually *welcome* it."

* * *

The house was one of those suburban McMansions. A sprawling three-story job that looked to have been built during the '90s boom, it was set on a hill and presided over several acres. An American flag hung from a pole in front.

"There's a nice surprise," Will said.

"You're not in New York anymore, my friend."

They turned up the long drive. "It looks like they've done all right for themselves."

Danny nodded. "On the other hand, these aren't New York prices. Place like this goes for just three-eighty, four hundred grand."

He said it with surprising authority, and Will shot him a look.

"Okay, what the hell? I made some inquiries. What, I'm supposed to think about the case every damn minute? I like Wisconsin. Who knows, I might end up out here."

"*Que te jodan*!" Will replied evenly, dredging up one of the PI's own pet phrases. "Really think I give a damn?"

The next surprise came as they walked toward the front door: a statue of the Virgin Mary in the garden, surrounded by carefully tended lilies.

"Traditional enough for you?" Danny said.

"Jesus Christ, I just hope I don't say anything to offend them!"

"You might start by not saying *that.*"

Almost as soon as they rang the bell, the Reichenbachs, both of them, were at the door.

Will was taken unawares. Seeing him, they betrayed no reaction at all.

"I'm so glad to see you," offered Laure, a slight, lilting French accent still there after all these years. She paused, gave a radiant smile. "You look taller than on TV."

Ah, so that's it! "Well, I try."

Though middle aged, she had the figure of a twenty year old and the face of, at most, a forty-three year old. Her husband Ed was somewhat older, probably on the wrong side of sixty, but he was a strapping six-two with muscles on muscles, and from the look of his heavily tattooed forearms, Will had no doubt he could toss a dwarf fifteen meters, no sweat.

"Great to see you, gents," Ed said. "Come on in."

They stepped inside the vast, sunlit entryway. Will gazed around. "Lovely place."

"It sure is," agreed Danny, who was also trying hard not to fixate on the gigantic bleeding Christ crucifix mounted on the wall.

"It's really too big for just the two of us," said Laure. "It can sometimes feel very cold and empty."

"Especially since the kids flew the coop," her husband added. "But, you know, it's close to our work."

"They run a gym nearby." Danny explained.

"Oh, I see."

"An Anytime Fitness Center," said Ed. "It's in Muskego, the next town over. But, you're right, that's just a glorified name for a gym."

"You know what I always say," said Laure. "'French women really don't get fat—at least not when they own a gym.'"

Their visitors laughed politely, and when she turned, both discretely sneaked a look at her ass.

"But, come," she said. "I know this is not why you're here."

She led them into the dining room. The was a table set for four with a large platter of cheeses in the middle, and Will was pleased to see there was a TV in the corner, silently tuned to an all-news station. But despite himself, he couldn't avoid staring at The Last Supper, which covered an entire wall.

"It doesn't bother you, I hope?" asked Laure, noticing.

"Of course not."

"Terrible, but this is a question one must ask these days,"

"No, I think it's beautiful."

Unexpectedly, she laughed. "You're funny. You think you have to be polite. Of course it is not great art. We know that."

Will nodded; a veteran connoisseur of BS, he was always ready to put his shit detector up against anyone else's, and it was rare indeed that his own phoniness stood so starkly revealed.

"But it gives us great comfort," said Ed.

"I'm sure," Danny said piously. "I'm not a religious man myself, but there are many, many times I wished I were."

"Exactly," Will quickly agreed, wishing he'd said it first. "Given the crumminess of the times."

"Well, never too late," said Ed, as they took their seats at the table. "The proof of that is right here before your eyes." He smiled. "I mean Laure and me, not the cheese."

"Edward," Laure said, cutting off the proselytizing with a gently admonishing glance. She turned back to her guests. "Speaking of which, these are all local, in honor of your visit." She pointed. "A cheddar cranberry... dunbarton blue... burrata... and my favorite, a Benedictine, made from a mix of sheep, goat and cow milk. Really, it's quite as good as those we have in France."

"The wine is also local," said Ed, reaching to the sideboard for a bottle.

"Only it's not," said his wife, smiling.

Will cast a quick glance at the TV, then looked back at them. "Sorry, I'm trying to keep an eye on my case."

She nodded. "We've been watching closely also; that's why it is on."

Will nodded his thanks. It was unusual for him to find such quick rapport with anyone, let alone people who under other circumstances he might've taken for proto-Martians. "Were you both raised Catholic?" he asked, spreading the cheese onto a slice of baguette.

"Not only Catholic, but by the nuns. I spent four years at a convent school." She laughed. "It nearly ruined me, and for years after I wouldn't go near a church."

"I was the same," Ed said. "In my childhood it just never took. And then, after that, it was the '60s and... well, it wasn't exactly the in thing."

"Or in the '70s, the '80s or the '90s," Laure added, with a wistful smile.

"And frankly, I was carrying some serious sins on my soul for a while there."

"Ditto," said his wife, though she pronounced it, charmingly, "Dee-toe."

To Will, himself a confirmed and irredeemable sinner, this talk of sin was more than a little odd, certainly not the sort of casual table talk he was used to. Then too, there was no telling where it might lead—like, for instance, to the fact, recorded in Danny's reports, that his charming hostess's past sins included a stint as what she would doubtless now describe as a fallen woman.

He followed up with Ed instead. "I understand you were once a Hell's Angel."

"Oh no, just a Baron. A lot of people can't tell the difference. We only tortured people sometimes, we didn't kill 'em." He laughed, though it wasn't clear he was joking, and took a sip of wine. "You're right, Hon; this wine is pretty bad."

"But then we found each other, and together we found our faith," said Laure. "Otherwise, who knows where we'd be today."

"Or if we'd even be alive."

There was a momentary silence. Will cast another quick glance at the TV screen.

"But I know you want to talk about Francine," she said, turning to Danny.

He nodded. "Right."

"I'm sure you were shocked by the news, as we all were," Will said.

"Well, fortunately we haven't seen her in many years," Laure said, "so I have nothing to say about her life recently. But yes, I will tell you all I can about the old days."

Will leaned forward. "Why 'fortunately'? Have you followed her work?"

"Her *work*—bof," she said scornfully, punctuating the sentiment with the uniquely Gallic expression of contempt.

"Some work," said Ed with disgust. "Anti-God and anti-America. To people like us, she was one of the ones wrecking—"

"No, Hon," she interrupted, for he seemed ready to go on in this vein quite a while. "Let it be; she's gone." They locked eyes and she nodded. "We must pity her. At this very moment her soul is burning in Hell."

Will allowed himself a small smile. That sounded pretty good to him.

But now, out of the corner of his eye, he caught sight of something happening on the TV screen: there were his brother and Kane, an anxious looking Arthur between them, making their way into the South Chester police headquarters through a frenzied crowd of shouting reporters. *Rival Professors Called 'Persons of Interest' in Grabler Death* read the words beneath.

Seeing his stricken look, Laure gently placed her hand on his arm. "Maybe what I have to tell you will help."

* * * * *

"So, okay, good," Danny said, all business, turning to her. "Let's talk about the old days, back in Madison. According to my research you moved in with Francine and another girl... Melissa."

"Yes."

"It would have been in early '82?"

"Oh, don't ask me, I'm so bad with dates."

"And at the time, you were supporting yourself, how?" Danny came right out with it, clearly testing her readiness to fully come clean.

"Turning tricks," she replied evenly. "I was young and very pretty. It was easy."

"You don't seem to have any problem talking about it," observed Will.

"Why would I? It was me, but you know, also not me. I was not a very happy person then."

"Angry and confused," Ed added. "Lost."

"Yes, lost... a lost soul."

"Would you say it was the same for the others?"

She looked upward, reflecting a moment. "No, not exactly. Melissa was a nice person, but weak. Easily dominated. She came from a rich family, and she was used to their telling her what to do."

"And Francine?"

Her tone hardened. "An angry girl, angry at the whole world. But a very strong personality."

Will nodded. *Some traits are pretty much cradle to grave.* "A leader, in other words."

She nodded. "And we were followers. Foolish and very weak." She shook her head. "She was bad for Melissa, and me too. Francine was mean, no conscience. Still, in the end it was our responsibility—"

"You're thinking about the arrest at the construction site." Danny said.

"Among other things... but that was the worst."

"What finally happened with that case? I couldn't find any records."

"Melissa's parents, Mr. and Mrs. Mayhew, they bailed us all out. Twenty thousand dollars each. But we decided not to show up for the trial."

"*Francine* decided!"

Laure turned to her husband and nodded. "That's what she said we should do. She said we should go underground instead. When we didn't show up for the trial, the Mayhews lost the money, but Francine said they were rich, so what did it matter?"

"And their own daughter agreed."

"She went along with it like she went along with Francine about everything."

"What about you?"

She hesitated, took a sip of wine. "I'm not proud of it, but yes, me too. I didn't want to go to jail. But right after that I moved out. I didn't want to be around them anymore."

"That's where I come in," Ed said, smiling.

"Yes, that's when we found each other." Reflexively, she looked up at the central figure in the painting. "And I thank Him every day."

"But you were still 'underground,' as you say."

She nodded. "I was. For four years." She looked at Ed. "We moved a lot, didn't we? All over the Midwest."

"At least half a dozen times. Illinois, Michigan...."

"With a different name every time, changing my hair color or wearing wigs. Back then it was simple to get a new birth certificate—just find someone around your age who died and say you lost the original. From that you could get everything else you needed, including a social security card. Melissa and Francine were doing the same thing."

"It sounds like a big game," Will said.

"Except you're always looking over your shoulder. It wears you down. I was always sure they'd catch me, especially with my French accent." She paused. "What's funny is I don't think they were ever really looking for me, I wasn't that important. When I finally turned myself in, they didn't even press charges." She smiled wistfully. "Wisconsin justice."

There was a long pause.

"Let me ask you, Laure," Danny said. "What were you hoping to find in that storage shed?"

"I think you already know, don't you? Dynamite... explosive caps."

"To be used for what?"

"Blow up buildings, destroy the infrastructure of the corporate state." She laughed mirthlessly at her own long-ago stupidity. "That was the idea, anyway. Francine said we were part of a great revolutionary army, one small part."

"But you never did—"

"No! *I* never did."

"And the others?"

She looked at Ed, who nodded.

"They did. They did bombings."

"Do you know how many?"

"Six or eight, at least. Corporation buildings and places that did animal experiments."

"You're sure of this?" Will asked. "Francine Grabler's participation can be verified?"

"We were in touch that whole period. We didn't see them very much, but we were in touch."

Will said, "Because, you know, if we go out there claiming Francine Grabler was a terrorist, a lot of people are going to be pretty skeptical." *Actually, they'll say we're fucking crazy.*

"I do not lie!" she said adamantly. "For years I was deceitful, yes, but I do not lie now. Never!"

It's not like her visitors needed to be convinced. What they'd heard only confirmed what they'd strongly suspected going in. Still, no question, it *would* be Will's ass on the line.

"All right," he said. "You say were in contact the whole time?"

"Wait!" She turned to her husband. "Edward...."

He nodded, got up and walked from the room. He was back in thirty seconds, carrying a cardboard box, the words *Manchester's On The Square, Madison* emblazoned in fancy script on the side.

"We are not crazy," Laure said, removing the top. "We would not say such things unless we have the proofs." She began removing items one by one and holding them up for inspection.

First came the wigs, scrunched up and otherwise misshapen after all these years: a jet black one, a red one, a blonde one. Laure fitted the last haphazardly on her head and laughed. "Chic, no?"

Next came glasses, nearly a dozen pairs in assorted styles, from old-fashioned wire rims to tortoiseshells. "These all have plain glass," she said. "Even then, I wore contacts."

Then came two pairs of cheap, thick-soled shoes, the sort worn at the time by price-conscious, fashion-indifferent middle-aged women, one in black, one in brown. "These!" she said. "Wearing them, it even changed my walk, which I thought was very clever."

This was all entertaining enough, but for practical purposes, useless. "Were any of these Grabler's?" Will asked, knowing that even if so, there'd be no way to prove it.

"No, all mine." She reached back into the box and pulled out a manila envelope. "But there is also this."

She turned it over and dumped the contents on the table: dozens of documents and cards, bearing a variety of names, all female.

"Some of these are mine, others theirs," she said. "They came by one night, unexpected. Francine seemed frightened, and told me to hold theirs. She said I was in less danger. So I put them in with ours." She paused. "She said she would come back for them, but she never did."

Will started to root through them. "What about her friend?"

She shook her head. "Just quiet, like always. Francine was the boss."

"Do you think they were maybe more than friends?" Danny asked delicately.

"Oh, no, I don't know about that. Not when I was there. Francine always had a lot of different men." She hesitated, looked at her husband. "Do you think that is possible?"

He shook his head. "I never saw anything like that. And didn't she have a child later?"

"*Francine Grabler?*" Danny couldn't hide the hint of a smile. "I never picked up anything like that."

Ed shrugged. "Just something I heard."

The cache was incredible: birth certificates; social security cards; driver's licenses—photos were not yet required—from states throughout the region; even department store credit cards, in a remarkable array of names. Amy Bronson. Susan McGill. Felicity Malen. Barbara Learnihan. Janet Poland. Nancy Follansbee. Rebecca Wheat. At least a dozen more.

But of course it was impossible to discern which young woman had assumed which identity, or for how long. The birth dates, when listed, would have had all of them in their mid-to-late twenties at the time, which reflected the actual ages of all three women.

"And these were also there," said Laure, seeming to guess what Will was thinking. She offered him two pieces of paper, and Danny leaned over to see as Will unfolded them.

The first was a map of the campus of McKinley College in Pembrook, Ohio, the sort given to prospective students and their parents. One building, labeled *Sanborn Hall*, had been circled in red, and there were arrows drawn that seemed to indicate the shortest route from the building to the main thoroughfare beyond the campus gate.

Will and Danny exchanged a meaningful look. The bombing of McKinley's ImmunoResearch lab was among those that had never been solved.

Will unfolded the second page, a sheet of standard yellow lined paper.

"Jesus!" Danny exclaimed involuntarily.

The page contained a just a couple of lines, but they were written in what he immediately recognized as Grabler's distinctive cramped hand.

Laure caught his look and nodded.

Will read aloud. "An explosive device will go off at Worthington Life Services labs after midnight on November 4. This is an action for humanity by the Wisconsin Women's Collective."

He turned to Laure.

"They always made a call beforehand, so there would be no casualties," she explained. "Always from a public pay phone. Francine made the calls."

"And Melissa?"

She gave a bitter laugh. "She put the bombs in the buildings." She paused. "When they were caught, that's why she went to jail, and not Francine—she took all the responsibility. Even though Francine picked the targets and gave the orders and did everything else."

Will nodded, it sounded like the Grabler he knew. "So when was the last time you saw them?"

"I visited Melissa just before she went to jail. She was out on bail. Her parents paid it again. Francine wasn't there. Melissa seemed very sad, full of regrets. She wanted to change her life. She told me she was writing a book."

"I Am My Own Father, Mother and Best Friend."

"I don't know the name, I don't think she had one yet. The thing that surprised me was when it came out, Francine's name was on the book also." She gave a knowing look. "Well, let's say I was surprised but not surprised."

Ten minutes later, Will and Danny were back in the entryway by the front door.

"I just have to ask you," Will said, as he shook her hand. "You've known this about Grabler all these years."

"That's right."

"And it's not like you were hard to find. Why hasn't it ever come out? I mean, she's been a controversial figure for a long time."

She seemed perplexed by the question. "You're the first ones to ever ask."

* * * * *

Will studied Martha Mayhew, on the couch across the room. Everything here at her Bridgeport place was just as Danny said—the beat up, second hand furniture, the shelves crammed with books, the general air of controlled chaos; everything, that is, but the woman herself. Danny had told him how reluctant she'd been to cooperate at first, and that even after he'd gotten her to start spewing, there remained a subtle undercurrent of tension, as if she was constantly aware of the possibility of saying too much. But here she was, feet curled behind her on the ratty couch, sipping chamomile tea, as relaxed as the mangy cat sleeping beside her.

"I liked your friend Danny very much," she said.

Will nodded. "He's down in Virginia wrapping up a few things." He paused. "He liked you too."

"Though it took me all of thirty seconds to figure out he was a private investigator and not a journalist." She smiled. "Quite a coincidence, him showing up, looking for dirt on Francine just when she was all over the news, throwing dirt at her rivals at Chester College. And that cock n' bull story about working for Con Ed—puh-leeze!"

Will hadn't touched his tea, but now he raised the cup in tribute, one scam artist to another. He couldn't wait to greet his colleague with the news; *she* played *you*, Danny boy, not the other way around.

"Either way," he said, "you were helpful, so I figured we owe you an update." He set down the cup. "Tell me, you knew Grabler as well as anyone—were you surprised how it ended?"

"You mean the way she died?" She hesitated a moment, seeming to tense slightly. "I guess I'd say nothing about Francine ever surprised me. But you know, I hadn't seen her in a very long time."

"But you were close once, it seems no one was closer."

"Well, you know, that relationship was *complicated*, let's put it that way. Because Francine herself was complicated."

He smiled. *Complicated.* Covered all manner of sins. Charlie Manson, he was *complicated*, and so was every psychotic mass murderer in history. "So," he said, moving to a subject area less fraught, "I understand you're a poet."

"I dabble," she said. "Nothing great, just okay. I've had a couple of things published in small magazines."

"Working on anything special now?"

"Not really."

He indicated her nearby work station, and the neatly stacked pile of printed pages alongside the computer. It was a good six inches high. "Looks like you have enough for a whole book."

"Oh that," she said, caught short. "It's just, you know, a personal project."

"You know, it occurs to me you didn't answer my question."

"What do you mean?"

"About Francine's death. Were you upset?"

She looked at him closely, as if trying to formulate an answer.

"Odd thing to have to think about. Okay, here's another one: Did she ever pay you anything for all those books you wrote for her?"

She stared at him another few seconds, but what he saw in her eyes was not so much panic as relief. "She was a friend. I helped her out."

"Right, it's *complicated.*" He smiled. "Lucky timing for Grabler—things fall apart between her and Hyatt-Sasaki, and there's her *friend*, fresh outta the clink, computer at the ready. Or wait, were you still using a typewriter back then?"

Mayhew responded with only the merest hint of a smile.

"Anyway, the good news is that now you might finally get to publish one under your own name."

"I doubt it," she said, the façade completely falling away. "It's always been her name that sold them. And it's the same book over and over, anyway."

"What did she have on you all those years, anyway?"

"What, you're going to pretend you don't know?" she said, fully aware now of who she was dealing with. "You saw Laure, right?"

He nodded. "A few days ago. Only because you steered us to Madison in the first place."

"How is she? I always liked her."

"She liked you too. She just thought you were weak."

She laughed, joylessly. "Well, she always was a straight shooter."

"It was the bombing in Eau Claire, wasn't it? The one where the janitor was killed?"

She closed her eyes, took a deep breath, and nodded.

"Wasn't Grabler always supposed to call beforehand to make sure the buildings were clear?"

"I still don't know what happened. That one time they didn't listen... at least that's what she said." She shook her head, and it was clear that she knew exactly what had happened.

"And I'll bet she had an airtight alibi for that night, witnesses up the wazoo."

She nodded. "And I was at a Motel 6 in Chippewa Falls, thirteen miles away, under a phony name."

"And there's no statute of limitations on murder."

As if she had to be reminded. "No."

"Well, your secret's safe with me," he said, zipping his lips. Hell, she'd already paid plenty, was still paying. "After all, you did hard time, anyway."

"Four and a half years in maximum security, the worst of my life."

"Where was that?"

"Taycheedah Correctional, outside Fond du Lac"

He waited a moment. "They had conjugal visits there, did they?"

Instantly, she knew where he was going. For the first time he saw something like terror in her eyes.

"Your son... he would've been born right in the middle of your stay there."

"Okay," she said softly. "Now you've got everything."

"He was Francine's."

She paused, she hadn't expected this part. "He was a year and a half when I got out. Francine had no use for him, she wasn't even sure who the father was. Her career was just starting to take off and she didn't want to be bothered."

"And you?"

"What career?" She smiled. "What life? I can't even say I regret it. He's given me something to live for."

"Does he know? Gregory?"

"He does. Of course."

"Did Grabler ever see him?"

"Almost never—and never in public. It didn't exactly go with her image." She gave a bitter laugh. "Did you read her last book?"

"So when she saw him, it was always in secrecy."

"Always. Those were her rules."

"Um hmm, I see." He waited a good ten seconds. "Like, for instance, in remote state parks?"

She just stared at him, a weird half-smile frozen on her face.

"I don't know," she allowed softly. "It's possible. He's been pretty messed up lately."

"I understand he's kind'a been stalking her, going to her readings."

"That was just... I don't know, to shake her up." She shook her head. "But yes, it's occurred to me."

"What better time, right? Right after she'd publicly confessed that she was emotionally devastated and possibly suicidal."

What was there for her to say? Now he really did know everything.

Of course, there were still the details: Was the kid a full-blown psycho or just a run-of-the-mill product of neglect? Was it all his doing or had Martha/Melissa used him as a murder weapon?

But truth be told, Will didn't much care about any of that. What mattered is that Grabler was history, and his clients were in the clear.

"Relax," he said. "No need to worry. Like they say, boys will be boys. Who's anyone to judge?"

* * * * *

Little more than week later, at precisely eleven a.m. on a Tuesday morning, Will was ready and waiting at his desk when the player piano in the outer office began tinkling "Alexander's Ragtime Band." President Frank was right on time.

A moment later, he walked through the door. "So," he said, smiling broadly. "We meet again."

Will nodded. “I’d get up, but I don’t feel like it.”

“That’s fine, that’s fine,” said Frank, his shit-eating grin in place, as he took the chair across the desk.

Will stared at him grimly, pleased; it was still early, but it was already looking like this would play out as he hoped. Just yesterday, he’d had Arthur hand deliver Grabler’s file to the president at his office in Chester, and a mere two hours later, his secretary had called to set this meeting. Now here he was, the SOB, making goo goo eyes across his desk.

Not that Will could blame him. The bill of particulars in the Grabler file, laid out one after the other, each fully documented, made for a devastating indictment. Her fraudulent academic credentials. The best sellers written by someone else that she’d published under her name. Her terrorist past, including her role as an accessory to murder. And, of course, it reflected not only on Grabler herself, but on the institution that had hired her, nurtured her, supported and profited from her work and, not least, scrupulously shielded her from scrutiny.

Who could tell what the fallout would be if they were made public?

Since Frank evidently had not brought his copy with him, Will pulled his own from the top drawer and wordlessly dropped it on the desk between them. More than three inches thick, it sounded with satisfying authority. It was all there: the sworn affidavits, the documents, the pieces of phony ID, even the opening chapter of one of Grabler’s books, with corrections in Mayhew’s hand.

“I presume you read it closely.”

"Closely enough." Frank was still smiling. "You're an excellent attorney, Mr. Tripp, I hope you don't think I've ever suggested otherwise."

"The woman was a complete and total charlatan. Uncredentialed. Practically illiterate! Pretending to decency and kindness with a background in terrorism and murder!"

Still, his visitor seemed nonplussed.

Will leaned forward, tapped the file. "It's all there. There is not even definitive proof she ever earned a high school diploma."

Frank gave a barely perceptible nod but remained silent.

"Frankly, this may just scratch the surface. Her claim on the CV to be a member of the Paspahegh Indian tribe of northern Virginia? If you'd spent even five minutes researching it, you'd have learned the Paspaheghs ceased to exist in the 18th century!"

"But she really *was* from Virginia," he countered, meaningfully.

"On to the recent events at Chester College itself. You've noted, I'm sure, that one of the student witnesses to Ms. Grabler's attack on her own property has now provided a sworn affidavit testifying as to what happened that night. You should know that the other witness stands ready to provide similar testimony."

"We are aware of that," he said. "And we will deal with it in due course."

Will wasn't sure he'd heard right. "Come again?"

"Through appropriate channels, of course."

"In brief," Will concluded, "the evidence confirms that every smear, calumny, defamation and aspersion cast by Francine Grabler and her confederates upon the good name and reputations of my clients was wholly false and without foundation."

"And your point is?"

Will stared at him a moment in disbelief. "Listen," he said, lying unashamedly, "I have no interest in embarrassing you or Chester College. Neither do my clients."

"Oh, don't worry about that," replied Frank amiably. "We don't embarrass easily."

Will was thrown, but tried not to show it; cynicism was *his* long suit; if nothing else, this guy was supposed to be a true believer. "What I'm interested in now is putting all this behind us, so the healing can truly begin."

Frank's face went red. "You're mocking me, Sir! That I will not tolerate!"

"And know what'll help the healing along?" Will got to his feet. "Money! We want lots of it! That's the kind of healing I'm talking about!"

"Healing is a sacred concept, not to be treated with disrespect!"

"And that's just for starters. Our other demands are as follows: one, that my clients be immediately reinstated to their faculty positions; two, that you provide each of them with a letter, signed by yourself, offering an official apology on behalf of Chester College for the shabby treatment they have received."

In fact, this was just tactical, to pump up the dollars. Kane had already informed Will that he'd had more than enough of the sick and sorry business of contemporary academia, and was retiring back home to Arkansas, and Bennett had pleased his brother by reporting he'd decided to go into private industry and start making an honest living.

But Frank didn't know that, and he looked troubled. "Mind if I sit behind the desk?"

"You want to sit behind *my* desk?"

"To consider your proposal. I think better that way."

Will made an extravagant sweeping motion. "Feel free."

Frank rose, taking Will's desk chair. Since the seat was unusually high to make up for Will's stature, he now loomed far above the other, especially when Will took the chair that Frank had abandoned.

"Okay," Frank said. "That's better." His brow furrowed. "Allow me to offer a counter proposal. Your clients will both quietly leave the school. If and when I am contacted by future employers, I will not make an issue of this sordid episode."

"You're out of your mind," Will said in outrage. "I demand that both of these extraordinarily gifted scientists and educators be reinstated forthwith!"

Frank shrugged. "I'm afraid that's not possible. They have already been replaced."

"By whom?" He paused. "What, by people whose skin color is better for your perverted purposes?!"

"That's right," he said, pleased Will understood. "Or whose genitalia."

Will took a moment to regain control, intent on not losing sight of his larger goal. Sure, he could publicly release the Grabler file, and get some cheap thrills as the story played out over a day or two. But the outrage, what there was of it, would soon fade. For what Frank had said was true: Chester, like so many other elite colleges cosseted by their own overweening sense of virtue and protected by a like-minded media, was beyond embarrassment on the basis of mere financial malfeasance, moral irresponsibility, or (if rooted in supposed idealism) murder—indeed, on *any* basis except the holy trinity of racism, sexism or homophobia.

Will was, above all, a realist, and the reality was that most of these places were beyond saving. But that didn't mean they weren't interested in *self*-preservation. He changed tact with an easy smile. "Tell me, do you know a Mr. Frederick Strauss?"

The color drained from Frank's face. Strauss was in charge of determining the final college rankings in the revered *USA Guide to American Colleges and Universities*, and for those in positions of power at such schools, there was no one to be feared more. "Why? Do you?"

"He's a friend." Actually, he was a tenant in one of Marty Katz's high-end buildings. "A copy of this file, plus information on how the school has dealt with this crisis, and now the fact that you are gutting two of Chester's strongest departments, will be delivered to his home this evening unless both men are formally reinstated before then."

"I really don't know how I can do that," he pleaded.

"All it would take is balls."

"Mine are tiny, hardly there at all, everyone knows that." He grinned hopefully. "I hoped you'd find that amusing."

"Not really."

"Please," he said, desperate. "Can't we discuss the other part of your proposal?"

Stony faced, Will looked up at him on his throne. "Three million dollars."

Frank didn't even hesitate. "Absolutely. Done."

Will could have kicked himself, the place's endowment was as rich as an Arab sheikdom. "Each."

He nodded. "That's what I assumed."

"I meant six."

In the end, they settled on four and a half million apiece, in addition to Will's fee, the costs of Danny's investigation, Barbara Ann's bar tab, and three quarters of a million each for Sergei and Khan for pain and suffering, plus full tuition to whatever institutions they transferred to.

"Good," Frank said, emerging from behind Will's desk. He offered his hand for a fist bump. "Healing. Give it up."

"I'll expect the checks tomorrow," Will said, ignoring him. "Make sure they're certified."

Frank started for the door, then turned back. "By the way, can I count on seeing you there?"

"Where?"

"At Chester, of course, on May 29th. We're very excited." Frank smiled his most engaging smile. "I made the decision personally. We'll be breaking ground for the Francine Grabler Center for Kindness and Advanced Oppression Studies!"

Will hesitated. Reaching into his pocket, he fingered the photo Danny had unearthed on his recent trip to Richmond, and brought along as his final bargaining chip. He was pleased now he hadn't had to use it. Taken by Claudia Mackey a few days before her friend Francine was to leave for junior college in Arizona, it showed Grabler beneath portraits of John Wilkes Booth, Lee Harvey Oswald and James Earl Ray. Steely-eyed, she stares directly into the camera, a Swastika armband on her upraised arm as she gives the Nazi salute.

"You said the 29th?"

He nodded. "Big day. *Huge.* It will be the largest such center in America, I expect full coverage in the national media."

Will returned Frank's smile, knowing now he'd be releasing the photo on the 28th.

"You kidding? Wouldn't miss it!"

~ Ends ~

ABOUT THE AUTHOR

Harry Stein is a writer and journalist whose work has appeared in a number of publications in which, given his current political views, he will surely never appear again, including *The New York Times Magazine*, *New York*, *Esquire* and *GQ*. Will Tripp, Pissed Off Attorney at Law is his first novel with StoneThread Publishing. His other StoneThread titles include *How I Accidentally Joined the Vast Right-Wing Conspiracy (and Found Inner Peace)* and *The Idiot Vote: The Democrats' Core Constituency*, an essay. Among his previous books are *No Matter What, They'll Call This Book Racist*, retitled *Why We Won't Talk Honestly About Race* for the forthcoming paperback. Others include *Ethics (and Other Liabilities)*, *One of the Guys*, *Eichmann in My Hands* (with Peter Malkin), *The Girl Watchers Club*, *I Can't Believe I'm Sitting Next to a Republican* and the novels *Hoopla*, *The Magic Bullet*, and *Infinity's Child.*

Made in the USA
Lexington, KY
29 July 2014